Were he a stranger, not allied to me,
Yet should I grieve for him.

Christopher Marlowe

WERE HE
A STRANGER

To Corc
whose mountain overlooks
this sea

WERE HE
A STRANGER

A Novel of Suspense

Mary Craig

Dodd, Mead & Company
New York

1 2 3 4 5 6 7 8 9 10

Library of Congress Cataloging in Publication Data

————————.
    Were he a stranger.

    I. Title.
PZ4.S56335We [PS3569.H85] 813'.5'4 78-19073
ISBN 0-396-07590-8

1

When John Fast plunged from the cliff into the surf at Big Sur, he was gone forever.

Later his wife, Sydney, learned that the Filanti brothers, trolling offshore, had seen the body fall. They had alerted the Coast Guard.

Later the sea yielded up an unsavory catch into the nets of the searchers, but John Fast was gone forever in a way that dead men seldom are.

That morning had begun like all others for Sydney Fast. She wakened to a progression of familiar sounds, John rustling into his running clothes, furtive against awakening her, and muted clatter from the kitchen below as he measured a precise amount of coffee to brew in his absence.

She smiled secretly at the soft whining of the dog as John let himself out into the dawn. If that Wagner were not so stupid, John could take him along. But the great Dane's compulsion to pursue any moving object made this impossible. At the flick of a deer's tail Wagner would abandon John, only to return hours later guiltily studded with ticks and foxtails.

At a quarter past seven Sydney stared the clock into focus. John would have finished the longest part of his daily run, reaching the point where his path merged with the highway above the surf that crashed against Big Sur. He would pause there, lean and gaunt, mopping his face and staring into the sea a moment before starting back.

Five miles. She twisted the shower head all the way over to bring hot water from the bowels of the house. Five miles John ran every morning. "It's good to push your heart," he told her. "Really make the old pump race."

"With a hangover?" she asked herself. "After love-making? In the rain?"

She turned her body like a spindle. Under the shower's blazing spray she planned breakfast. Croissants from the freezer, eggs in the shell, and some casaba that was remarkably good for so late in the season.

The grandfather clock in the downstairs hall chimed eight while she toweled herself.

By the time the clock chimed again, she was conscious that John was running late.

With everything waiting, she went to gather asters for their table. She stared at the path leading to the cliff, momentarily expecting John's blue-clad figure to emerge from the dense woods.

Instead she heard a siren wailing. If there was a fire, she should see a pillar of smoke rising somewhere. But a fire would at least explain John's tardiness. The boy in John would stop to look, and the man in John would stop to help. But it was strange that she could see no sign of smoke above the trees in any direction.

The asters resisted being arranged in the black bowl she had selected. Then there were the dead leaves to clear away. Her growing annoyance at John made her awkward. She dropped the wadded leaves on Lena's immaculate kitchen floor and had to clean them up again.

"You have really become adjusted to this life," she told herself, half amused. "John is a little off schedule and you can't handle the change."

Getting used to the solitude of the house John had built her on this hill had not been easy. She had been forced to train herself to it consciously. Always before there had been people about her. On this hill she had only John and the housekeeper, Lena, coming and going and lately the dog, Wagner.

I have become more of a hermit even than John, she admitted, setting the finished arrangement on the table. She had ranged the house like a sullen child when John had gone on that rare trip to San Francisco this past summer. She had been affronted when he brought the dog home without discussing it with her first. She had even resented the way Lena had changed lately under the influence of a new friend whom Lena mentioned constantly—it was "Pilar this," and "Pilar that."

And all of this was so ridiculous. She had married John knowing what she was doing. She had accepted the sanctuary of his greater age and his silent strength. John was safety. Being John's wife was an identity she had assumed gratefully.

But her resistance to change was making this exceptional morning painful.

Impatient at the door, staring into the woods, she heard the pulse. It was a familiar enough sound, that helicopter thrumming over the ocean, the rhythm coming from the south, the direction that John had taken too long ago. Fear.

3

"Wagner," she shouted. "Wagner, walk."

There was nothing wrong with John, she told herself as she slid the choke chain over the Dane's uplifted head. Some fisherman had brought his boat in too close to shore. Nothing could have happened that concerned John out running as he always did, five miles every morning, fog or sun.

Wagner crashed tail and hip against the door in his haste to be outdoors. His spittle gleamed on the polished floor as he panted his enthusiasm.

Dark birds lived in the junipers. They twitched alarm as Wagner tugged her along John's running path.

She kept herself angry at John for worrying her. Somewhere up there they would run into him, and he would have to walk back with them slowly, with Wagner heeling at his side with assumed docility.

Wagner slowed as they approached the curve where the path went straight up to the cliff.

The crash of surf tunneled up past her, muting the sound of the helicopter to a fainter insect sound behind its clamor.

Then she saw the men, five or six of them. From the open doors of two police cars, radios chattered. One red signal light blazed futilely into the brighter sun of morning.

She clung to Wagner's lead as she searched for John. Not seeing him, she approached slowly, tightening Wagner's lead against her side. The policeman who approached her looked blurred somehow, his features fused into a vagueness by the suddenness of her fear.

"What are you doing?" she asked. "Why are you here?"

"Accident." He was terse. "You live around here?"

She nodded. "I came to meet my husband," she explained. "He is walking."

She saw their exchange of glances and a surge of movement towards her, as if to support her.

The policeman's face was firm, but his eyes on hers were withdrawn. He had retreated into some memorized place. He recited slogans to her like idiot cards at a broadcast.

"Accident," he explained. "Hit-and-run driver. Victim went off here." He pointed to tire tracks that swerved toward the edge of the cliff. "Some fishermen saw him fall."

The pulse that was almost drowning his words was not her own. The helicopter was nearer, circling.

"Accident," the man repeated, shouting against the din. "Driver must have lost control. Sharp curve here."

"John was jogging," she said dully. "It couldn't have been him. He was just jogging."

"Past here?" he asked.

The tires had cut a deep pattern into the fog-moistened earth. Beyond them was only sky above sea. Wagner complained at the pressure on his choke chain.

She did not look down. Stones rose from there like crusted spires. In among them foamed the ocean, tugging at the stubbornness of mussels and slowly wearing away the pillars of stone.

The policeman stared at her until she looked up. He seemed to be receding. How could he do that, look as if he were going away and yet remain the same size, sturdy in his heavy stitched blue clothing?

"And you say your husband never came back from his run?" he asked.

"It can't be John," she told him.

"But he didn't come back?" the policeman pressed.

"No," she admitted. At the sound of her own word she began to tremble. Fear pressed on her from the helicopter throbbing towards shore again.

The fear moved through her body and into her legs. Suddenly she was running. This time she stayed ahead of Wagner, dragging the big dog along. She heard the man call after her, but she didn't look back. She tried to shout "No" at him again, but the wind whipped the word flat against her face, making it sound more like a moan than a reply.

2

Once inside the house, Sydney was sorry she had run. It hadn't made any sense for her to run away like that. That policeman might think that it was John who had fallen from the cliff, but he was wrong. Impossible. But since it could not be John, she had been silly to run away like that.

Wagner was frantic with thirst. The cave of his lungs rose and fell in gasps. She ran the water cold before filling his bowl. She kneeled to watch him drink. His tongue looped torrents of water that splashed them both.

"I shouldn't have run away," she told Wagner finally, out loud.

Wagner rolled his eyes at her but didn't stop drinking.

An acrid odor from the burned coffee that John had put on so long ago filled the house. Sydney emptied the pot and finished filling it with a strong soda solution just as the doorbell sounded.

The policeman looked apologetic and cross both at once. His hair was damp under the edges of his cap. He looked planted on her porchway like a well-pruned tree. The only small things about him were his hands, square with those short fingers that suggest greediness at table.

"I'm sorry to bother you, Miss . . . Mrs. . . ." He had a pad out in his hand. "I knew right off that we startled you."

She backed into the hall, motioning him towards the living room, whose windows angled onto the sea. "It's all right, I guess. I just wasn't thinking straight. Seeing all of you there and all." She faltered before going on. "That man down there couldn't be John."

"Then he's here?" he asked, looking bewildered.

She kept her voice firm. "No, he's not here yet, but that still can't be John."

His eyes strayed from her. "I need to ask you some questions," he said.

She sat on the divan so that he would quit teetering in the doorway, looking like an upright log about to fall on something.

"You say your husband was jogging?"

"Is jogging," she corrected stubbornly. "They haven't found anyone yet, have they? How do you know that the fishermen didn't make the whole thing up? People do things like that, you know. And even if there was a man, there's no reason for you to think it was John."

He wrote down the "John" patiently, waiting for her burst of petulance to be over.

"They haven't found the body yet," he conceded. "But this is my job. People report. I investigate. Right?"

Chastened, she asked, "What do you want to know?"

"Your name and your husband's." He smiled, trying to be winning. "Just for starters."

"His name is John Fast, Junior, and I am Sydney Fast." She wondered if she should add the Doctor and decided it would be confusing. That "doctor" was important to

8

John, but there were lots of people who thought only of medicine with the term. She shrugged. "John Fast, Junior," she repeated. He looked up, surprised at the repetition.

"And this is your place?"

She flared with annoyance. Place. What a stupid way to put it. All right, it was his job to investigate, not to be skillful with words.

"This is our home," she said firmly, not caring if she embarrassed him.

"And how long have you lived here?" He glanced at the mitred beamed ceilings, the long expanse of sea visible beyond the windows.

"Five years," she said slowly, realizing. "Five years and a week to be exact."

He nodded, as if approving her exactness. The questions droned on and she answered them automatically. Through his words she measured the minutes by the strokes of the hall clock. She heard the back door open a little after nine. Lena was entering quietly because she was late. Sydney heard Wagner's whimper of welcome and Lena soothing him quietly. Lena probably thinks this is John in here with me, she realized suddenly. She will come down the hall, her arms full of dusters, expecting John.

The patrolman was silent. His unheard question hung in the air as he waited for her attention to return to him.

"I'm sorry," she said. "Did you say something?"

"Is that the maid?" he asked.

"The housekeeper," she corrected. "Lena Jensen, from the valley."

He nodded, writing that down, too. "How often does she come?"

9

"Five days a week, but I don't see why it matters to you. Why aren't you out there on the cliff with your radio? What can you do here that will help that man . . . if there is a man?"

He raised his eyebrows, as if her words pained him.

"Only one thing more. What was your husband wearing when he left to go jogging?"

"A dark blue warm-up Head suit," she recited. "White socks and Tretorn shoes. They were brown—a russety kind of brown, like dead leaves."

"You saw him leave?"

"No," she said, crossly again. "I was asleep, but that is what he always wears for jogging. Every morning, five miles."

"How about his family?" he asked.

"He hasn't any family."

"None that you know of at all?"

Sydney absorbed his implication levelly. What oblique glimpses she had caught of John's life before their marriage had been into a cold and nameless world. Still she resented his putting it like that.

"And your own family?" he asked, apparently resigned to her silence about John.

"No," she said. "No family at all."

He looked at her quizzically before rising. Guilt caught at her throat. But a family was an operating communicative group. If he had asked about relatives, she might have been more candid.

He stopped again in the hall. She felt Lena in the kitchen doorway, watching. He hesitated briefly. "Don't make too much of this, Mrs. Fast. I'm mostly just curious. Does your husband have any enemies?"

She stared. "Why do you ask?"

10

"At first we thought a driver lost control on that curve. Now it looks more like a car was parked up there for quite a while, waiting. Then it started quickly and struck the walking man."

"That's wild, and you know it," she said. "John had no enemies, no enemies at all."

She slammed the door, leaving him standing there on the other side of the sound. He had tricked her. She was angry and bitter about that. He had tricked her into suggesting that the man in the sea (was there a man in the sea at all?) was John.

She stood inside the door because there was no other place to go. She wasn't going to cry. She wasn't going to go to pieces because John was late. But where was he?

The policeman's question about enemies had caught her off guard. She herself had entertained questions. Her doubts had all come recently, each one because of some strange thing that John had done. Late in summer he ordered all the locks on the house changed, installing ugly chain bolts on the outside doors. They rattled and clanked like prison doors when she went in and out. He had made a lone business trip to San Francisco that had been almost mysterious. He had come back too tired, his face darkly shadowed. And buying Wagner. John had never defined Wagner as a watchdog, but he was obviously trained for that and John had been insistent on leaving him loose to range in the house at night.

It was silly of her to think about these things. She had confronted John about his precautions, and he had laughed. "Old men are cowards," he explained. "As your supply of time diminishes, your vigilance increases."

Lena was still waiting, her thinned eyebrows straining

11

towards each other with concern. Once those brows had been thick and bushy, giving Lena's face a nice solidity. But Lena's new friend, Pilar, had persuaded her to pluck them out, so that Lena looked strangely unbalanced with a straggling line of hairs above her round eyes, which glittered now with curiosity. But her tone was gentle. "You all right?"

Sydney nodded. "Something strange has happened."

Lena's heavily painted lips tightened against her gums. "I heard in town. My car wouldn't go again and had to be towed down to the station. I should have taken your car like Mr. Fast said I should, but instead I got into being late again."

"Never mind being late," Sydney told her. "What did you hear in town?"

"That them Filanti brothers were fishing off the cliff when they saw a man fall. They brought their boat in fast and made the report. The Coast Guard got out right off. At the station they talked about suicide."

Sydney shook her head. "A car was up there. They think the man was run off."

"How could they know?"

"They couldn't," Sydney admitted. "They're only guessing." Suddenly a broad range of possibility spread before her. There were options, brightly lit with a sanguine light of hope.

"Just think, Lena. Maybe the man had been murdered or something in the car and they dumped him off there. Maybe they had to struggle with him if he wasn't already dead."

Lena retreated behind the darkness of her small eyes. Doubt thickened her heavy lower lip as she stared at Sydney. "What does Mr. Fast think?"

Sydney started bravely but then faltered. "He's ... he's not here, Lena. He went out jogging and hasn't come back yet."

Sydney watched Lena's open face grow furtive. "Shouldn't you lie down or something?" the housekeeper asked.

"I'm not an invalid," Sydney said. "Why should I lie down half way through the morning?"

"Until he comes," Lena explained, retreating a little. "That's a lot of shock for a body to have, a policeman coming and all."

Sydney tightened her lips and stared at Lena, startled at the change in the woman.

Lena was a flat person, a paper doll woman with a narrow tunnel of a life. Sydney knew Lena's husband, Lars. He was a great eyebrowless face trimmed with tufts of pale hair. He worked night shift doing something that lifted small patches of dry skin on the backs of his hands. He spoke in a monotonous singsong, his voice rising to questions where none were implied. Even the children who tumbled about their house out there in the valley were indifferently shaped, with pale, anonymous faces.

Now Lena was becoming a real person. The phenomenon was startling. This was a replay of the "Sorcerer's Apprentice," a broom suddenly flashing with life and beginning to dance. Lena fumbling at psychology? Lena assuming a sudden control? It was incredible. Irritation burned in Sydney's throat, making her swallow with effort.

"You're probably right." She was Wagner suddenly, all her power chained by a circumstance she couldn't claw off. Like Wagner under the choke, she pretended docility. "You'll tell me when John comes?"

13

3

Up in her room with the solitude she had arranged, Sydney felt trapped. She tried to watch the search from the upstairs balcony, but the angle of the hill was wrong. She heard only the steady pulsing of the helicopter and at long intervals the voice of the clock from downstairs.

Almost viciously she slammed the French doors to escape that sound and the sight of a sea whose glaze seemed suddenly perilous. Now there was only the time and the quiet of her room and John's.

She hadn't wanted to marry him.

"I don't see that it is necessary," she told him. "Marriage could spoil things for us. We could just go on like before." She had smiled to coax him. "An intangible beginning and an intangible end."

He hadn't smiled back. "I am a man used to compacts." She had been annoyed at his choice of words. Another man would have said "contract." *Compact* was a stultifying word, tight and concentrated. She imagined great masses pressed down by time and therefore changed. "Anyway," he added, a little more lightly, "all things have beginnings and ends. With marriage, the middle is enriched, at least."

She wanted to ask how marriage could enrich the easy pleasure of what they had, but their words had gone away into touch and then laughter. But the smaller compact within that marriage was that past time didn't exist for them. "We begin together," he said almost fiercely. "I want no part of past time."

With a cold cloth on her head, she lay on John's side of the bed thinking about John, about the questions that the policeman had asked.

Just remembering his words irritated her. What if she had disappeared instead of John? How would John have answered those questions? "No family," he would have said, just as she had. He knew vaguely that there were people behind her, that there had been a place that had formed what he knew as Sydney, but he had never probed it.

In the very beginning, he had laughed at her a lot. "My God," he had cried, "where did you come from, anyway?" She had not known what answer he sought. She knew it wasn't Iowa that he wanted to hear, so she just shrugged.

"You're so . . . cool," he had decided out loud. "Isn't there anything you want a lot—enough to, say . . . fight for it or sell your soul for it?"

"I'm not very brave," she had confessed.

"Courage hasn't anything to do with it."

"Of course it does," she had remonstrated, wondering at the moment how she dared contradict her own college professor. "Cowards don't push . . . for fear of getting pushed back."

"What are you afraid of?" he asked curiously.

She had not been able to answer him. She hadn't really known what she was afraid of. Now that she knew, there was no one there to explain it to.

One dream had come again and again to her when she was younger. She knew she was asleep even as she lived in the dream. She knew that if she could waken, the dream would leave, taking its terror with it, but she never had strength enough to pull herself from the open place that was her dream. She stood in clear, bright air that cast no shadows. Even her size was puzzling, because there was no point for comparison. And the light always grew brighter, melting her body away in waves of shimmer. She clasped herself frantically with her arms, feeling herself turn to nothing in her own grasp. Because she was not defined she did not exist. She could remind herself fiercely of all the things she had been in different corners of her life: the good child, the capable student, and, finally, John's wife. But in that exposed dream, she became nothing. As the light dimmed, she became a shadow among shadows, voiceless and nameless.

"I am afraid of not being," she said aloud in the empty room. For fear that the dream would come, she forced her mind to other things to keep her from sleep.

The policeman. What if the policeman was right and the man who was driven from the cliff was John?

Guilt. "But I have been a good wife," she whispered defensively. "I have been thoughtful and responsive. I have been tender and loyal." My God, it sounded like a Boy Scout oath, she realized bitterly. She had been all the things that a good wife or a good scout should be, but she knew that she had never given any inner part of herself to John. Her life with John had been like a war against the dream. She had made herself, in that walking sleep, into the good wife so as to define who she was. But who had John been while she dreamed through this marriage?

"A happy man," she told herself fiercely. "I have made John happy."

The exhaustion of waiting and listening finally brought a sleep unhealthy with phantoms.

She wakened to darkness with a rectangle of light widening from the dimly lit hall. She sprang up with panic.

"Lena?" she asked of the silhouette against the light.

"It's me, all right," Lena's voice was soothing. "You slept."

Lena turned on the lamps, one and then the other, always with her back to Sydney.

"There's a man to see you," she said.

Then John had not come. She didn't want to see any man but John.

"It's late, Lena," Sydney realized aloud. "It's after six."

"I called Lars. It's all right that I am staying."

"But it isn't necessary," Sydney protested. "What about the children?"

Lena laughed. "Pilar is right there. And she'd rather fool with those kids than eat. She's got none of her own, you know. She'll just run over and take care of them."

"Then she's a neighbor," Sydney said as she rose. Pilar had always been confusing to her. She had seemed to appear all of a sudden as a force in Lena's life. Pilar advising this, Pilar suggesting that. Sydney had only seen Pilar once when the woman left Lena off at the gate. Her impression was of a dark, threatening foreignness that had made Sydney retreat into the doorway to wait until

17

the flamboyant creature had gone. Spanish, Lena had said.

"You might say she's a neighbor." Lena laughed. "Lars had her trailer moved right in there by our back door so he could hook on lights and water. Couldn't be more convenient."

Sydney pulled the brush through her hair and walked woodenly down the stairs.

4

"Don Sexton," the man before her fire announced, extending his hand and a leather folder rather like an Italian wallet. "I'm investigating the accident on the cliff." As he flipped the wallet open, she waved it away.

"I believe you," she told him.

Her mind was not behaving sensibly. Maybe it was because she hadn't eaten and had only slept away all those tormented hours. Her mind could not pass his name. Sexton. Why send a man with such an ominous name to talk to her? There was a poem. Not a nursery rhyme, but something later than that. The first lines came easily, "His death which happened in his berth at forty-odd befell." She frowned to recapture the rest of it, the part about the sexton,

> "They went and told the sexton
> And the sexton tolled the bell."

Thomas Hood, she remembered, with a small sense of triumph.

"I'm sorry, she said, pulling her mind back. "I was distracted by your name."

"To most people it suggests black beetles," he admitted, smiling. "But you must have heard a lot of word play on your name, too."

She nodded. "The gamut from classical to racy. You have something to tell me?"

He had a good face. His expression went from humor to gravity swiftly. She wondered idly how they chose police inspectors. The police were always there, working in the woodwork of the world, pulling drivers off for citations, keeping intersections sporadically cleared. When the police recruited a detective, did they specify a man with a clean line of jaw and a flexible face? "Must be able to smile or shout fiercely without disfigurement."

"I have some questions," he said into her reverie. "Can we go back to the beginning?"

Her face wanted to smile but she didn't let it. Go back to the beginning? Indeed, Mr. Sexton, do you have time? Seven years? Can you imagine the casual sensual ease of a beginning, the panic of commitment, and finally this ghost-ridden day?

"You must mean this morning," she corrected him.

She had the unfortunate feeling that he understood her.

"We need to start with this morning," he agreed.

"It was like all other mornings," she explained. She watched him absorb John's rising into half darkness, his prescribed five-mile jog with the sky still dark above the pale sea.

"Nothing was different?" he asked.

She shook her head.

"Nothing was bothering him? There were no enemies he feared?"

"The other man asked that."

"I have to ask again."

She thought of the new locks and Wagner.

"Not that I know of," she replied. "What about the man that the fisherman reported?"

"We recovered the body," he told her. "Late this afternoon."

He waited momentarily before going on.

"The victim was a man in his early to mid-fifties, about six feet tall, a hundred seventy pounds, dark hair showing some gray, brown eyes. He had an old healed surgical scar on the right rib cage. Severe recent contusions on the left side of his body indicated that he was struck forcibly by a heavy object shortly before his death."

"And that killed him?"

"The autopsy established drowning in sea water as the cause of death."

Autopsy. She was suddenly aflame with fury. "How did you dare? How could you presume to drag a man out of the sea and carve him up?"

"We had no choice," he said. "There was the evidence of the waiting car, the tracks by the cliff. When there is a possibility of murder, we need positive identification as well as cause of death."

"So you come back with a description," she said. "The streets are crowded with tall, graying men in their fifties. A lot of good your butchery did you."

"We also got fingerprints, dental charts. We have other things," he went on quietly. "The man was legally identified as Graham Hastings."

She had steeled herself for his words and then they came wrong. Something warm and sweet seemed to flow along her limbs. He stopped her cry of relief with a raised hand of caution.

"He was wearing a blue Head warm-up suit," he went

on, "and one shoe like the pair you described to the policeman."

"But it wasn't John," she insisted. "You said . . . another name."

"Graham Hastings," he repeated. "Have you ever heard that name before?"

"Never," she said sullenly.

John was not dead. Never mind the long arm of coincidence that had dragged another man from life into the sea, in those same clothes, that same size and coloring. John was not dead.

"Did your husband live under an alias?"

"No, of course not," she flared. "What is all this? You're only human you know—you can make errors. That dead man is not John, but even if he were, he would *be* John . . . not this other . . . this Graham Hastings."

"You're not thinking this through," he reminded her. "This is a solitary place. Your husband was running—"

"Jogging," she corrected him fiercely. Running sounded like escape, like hiding under a false name.

"Jogging," he repeated. "He was jogging along that cliff. The victim's description matches that of your husband, and your husband is missing. We can only draw the conclusion that the dead man, Graham Hastings, and John Fast are the same man.

"You are the only one who can help us," he added.

"But I don't know," she replied stupidly. If John Fast and Graham Hastings were the same man, then John was dead. They didn't expect her to accept that, did they?

"Then I would file a missing person's report, Mrs. Fast. Either way you need to know and we need to know."

"You think this man in the sea was murdered?"

"In any case, you need to come to identify him."

"Do we have to go now?"

"We should." His tone was measured. "Time is important in an investigation of this kind."

There he was, using a generic phrase, implying that every day men were forced into the sea by waiting cars. She bit her lip as she rose from her chair.

"You must have a close friend, some family who'll come along," he suggested.

"You are sure it is John, aren't you?" she challenged him.

"I'm trying to help you," he replied.

"There's nobody," she said fiercely, starting into the hall.

She had forgotten Lena. But Lena was holding Sydney's leather jacket. She had brought Sydney's shoulder bag from the closet upstairs. Lena's eyes were softened by weeping. Why should Lena weep? But this was an altogether irrational day. The fire behind her crackled suddenly, exploding a fan of sparks behind the bronze screen. Sydney stared back at it as she slipped her arms into the jacket Lena held.

"I'm coming, too," Lena told Don Sexton, shoving her arms awkwardly into the sleeves of the shabby tweed coat she always wore to work. Her bellicose expression anticipated argument.

"That's good," he said quietly. "That's very good."

"You don't have to go through this, Lena," Sydney told her.

"I called Lars already," she explained.

"Thank you," Sydney remembered to say. It would be

graceless to refuse the girl's thoughtfulness. Could Lena be expected to know what John and she had known about solitude?

"How many people stir about doesn't matter," John had said. "Alone is alone is alone."

"Shades of Gertrude Stein," she had kidded.

"Shades of man against the abyss," he had replied. "Or maybe the man against the darkness of his own shadow."

The jacket sleeves felt cold and inhospitable against her arms.

"Is it possible that Graham Hastings had enemies?" she asked.

Don Sexton stopped in the doorway and regarded her. "Most men do," he replied. "He was born in Georgia in 1923. His people were well-known bankers in Atlanta. He went into the army in 1941, served four years in Europe, and was honorably discharged in 1945."

"And his family?" she asked.

"No record of marriage," he replied. "Father and mother both dead, a couple of aging aunts left, and a cousin of about his own age named Lee Railland still in the bank there."

She fell silent. This was so ridiculous. John Fast was a teacher; there was no trace of a southern accent in his voice. Aunts? A cousin his own age? Coincidence had plunged this other man into their stretch of sea. 1923, Don Sexton had said. John was born in 1923, on the 23rd of October. In just a couple of weeks they would have John's annual birthday dinner.

"Blessed is he who is born in the season of the crab," John always said, laughing. She would fix artichokes with oysters and a salad, then just the steamed crab with drawn butter and lots of sourdough bread. She used to fix dessert, too, but had given that up. They never ate it anyway, not after all the Blanc et Blanc and the good talk.

Sydney moved away from Don Sexton, toward the door. He moved swiftly to hold it open for her the way John always had, with his body between her and the wind that blew in from the sea. Lena was following, her eyes careful on the redwood rounds. Sydney ran up the stairs ahead of them, drawing confidence from her intimacy with the stones and the brush of plantings against her legs.

The harvest moon rolled up over the headlands in a blaze of muted rose. It would fade as it climbed higher, cleansing itself of the earth until it was a translucence, so thinly stretched that the sky would show through its face. Rose to gray. Sydney pulled her jacket closer. Like people fading with age until their only color was the gray pattern of time etched on their faces.

They rode in silence with only the even humming of the car engine as they wound along the twisting highway. Lena was still silent when Don Sexton led them down polished halls that echoed at their passing.

Lena's mind seemed locked in behind her flat face like a dormant animal. When Sydney touched her hand, Lena turned to her with a startled expression.

"Thank you again for coming," Sydney said.

Lena's face darkened as she shook her head, her eyes glinting with moisture.

Sydney stared at the corpse they produced. It was so still that even the memory of life had faded from it. The hair was combed all wrong. That face, that even in sleep had pulsed with silent dreaming thought, was slack and passive.

John Fast had been a teacher, she reminded herself. She remembered his frowning concentration when lecturing, the glitter of excitement in his eyes at the turn of an argument in the pale wintery light of a classroom fetid with cigarette smoke and the muskiness of old books.

And a lover. It was then that she looked away. John Fast had fled, leaving this waxen effigy.

She toyed with the idea of lying. She could state coldly that the man they had drawn from the sea was not her husband. It would be Lena's word against her own— Lena and some small cluster of people who had seen them come and go and chatted casually with them over Irish knits or loaves of fresh bread.

She would not even be lying, really. John was too vital a creature to lie this still. But the lie would be pointless. There was no lie audacious enough to bring John Fast swinging back through the pines with Wagner straining against his leash, nor to restore the scent of his flesh to her pillow.

She turned away and went out the door, past Don Sexton and Lena, standing awkwardly beside him.

"You were right," she said. "John Fast is dead."

Don Sexton would have said something to her, but she stopped him with an impatient shake of her head.

"I want to go home," she told him.

The card by the corpse read "Graham Hastings." But John Fast was dead, too, so finally that Sydney stumbled on the polished stairs, having lost any sense of herself even as she did inside that dream.

5

The days that followed were formless. A darkness of disbelief hung over them. The clock in the hallway stopped time and released it with monotonous regularity, but time itself ceased to move forward. It was emptied of progress or promise.

Sydney made a puppet of her body and dressed it and painted its face and set it moving. The puppet was docile and proficient. She watched it with wry satisfaction. How punctually it walked Wagner along his trails, how tidily it made arrangements for that body which the catalyst of death had changed from John Fast to Graham Hastings.

Her mind that had swung free in that darkness became less manageable. It darted like a captured bat in an unfamiliar place. Even while the puppet watched clods of clay fall heavily on John Fast's casket, her mind moved among the flowers banked there, storing their coolness, bathing in their color.

Lena's family came to the funeral. Lena wept and Lars vibrated from some inner river of grief that moistened his eyes and his nose and thickened his voice. Their children's puzzled eyes darted like chipmunks among the alien stones. She recognized some tradesmen with whom

27

she and John had done business and a sprinkling of casual acquaintances from Carmel. Don Sexton was there. Sydney was relieved that he looked troubled instead of grieving. Hypocrisy was not the light she wanted shed in the dark place where she moved.

A lot of things didn't grow anymore in that darkness. Her energy simply went away. With it went the rage that had blossomed the morning John was killed.

"I am a slug on a leaf," she told Wagner. "I am safe only until the wind blows the leaf away." Her mind and body fused into a torpid union. The Monday she went for groceries she saw pumpkins on porches along the street. She heard two customers in the store discussing politics. She was incredulous that this time still had seasons and that other tragedies played inanely on other boards.

Maybe she would end like this, she mused, slowing down steadily until everything would stop altogether and there would be only the darkness and the silence left.

She even accepted changes in her house. Wagner, who had once slept with a sodden completeness, became a night prowler that very first night that John was gone. Sydney would waken to his restless padding along the halls and through the downstairs rooms. She ceased to startle with alarm when he shattered the night silence with agonies of barked warning. "There is nothing out there," she told herself. "Wagner simply misses John the way I do." So she called him to her and slept with one hand resting lightly on the warm twitching smoothness of his back.

6

Don Sexton had energy enough for both of them.

He sent a driver for her and set her in a room that was pregnant with listening.

They told her she need not answer any questions she did not want to. That she could have an attorney present if she wished. That everything she revealed to them could be used against her.

She knew the statement came from the law, but it didn't seem relevant. She felt that their questions rose from some remarkable vigor, but she could not figure out what they expected the answers to yield. She puzzled at this only mildly, since she had nothing to conceal.

An old man with white hair and glasses too large for the size of his skull recorded her words. He seemed altogether lifeless. Only his fingers were animated, moving vigorously on his instrument with a steady drumming sound.

Stripped of the warmth of life, she gave them the bones of her life with John.

"You were his student?" Mr. Sexton asked almost cordially. "And after that his wife?"

She nodded.

"And after you were married you travelled?"

"And after travelling you built this house here?"

"What was your husband's business?"

"He had no business."

"But what about his teaching?"

"When he was teaching he was a teacher. After that he was my husband."

It was clear that they didn't understand her, but it didn't matter. She spoke fact and the keys of that rattling machine were obviously tailored for fact. She owed it no more.

"But you had to have money," he argued. "It takes money to travel, to build houses like that," he waved his hand expansively.

"Of course there was money. He was bright enough to have made very good investments. He used to tell me not to worry, that time generally ran out before money."

"And that money is now yours?"

She shrugged. "I suppose so."

"And how much money is there?"

"I don't know."

"And you haven't checked? Was there a will? Insurance?" Frustration moved behind his voice as she looked back at him.

"I haven't checked."

"Then you knew before?"

"No," she said, daring him to challenge her.

"Friends," he suggested, willing her to name people from her life to fit this category.

She only shook her head.

"Family?" he asked with exasperation.

"I left home a long time ago," she replied. "Before John."

Slowly the pattern of the questions made her wary. They weren't asking for information, she decided. They were trying to shape something from her monosyllables. And the shape of what they sought chilled her.

Even after the silent driver took her home she refused to believe that they really thought she had killed John. It was too ridiculous a thing for them to suggest.

But not even her torpor could protect her from those questions. Whole blocks of their questions haunted her when she was apart from them. Fragment by fragment the weight of their suspicions grew in her mind, insidious tendrils into the corners of her self-knowledge.

There was that stupid business about the tire tracks.

Like serious children with plasticene, they produced a model of the tire tracks where the car had waited on the cliff. They expounded about weight and time and gave their educated opinion as to how long the car had sat there . . . waiting.

With triumph, they produced a model of the tracks of the red Corvette that she and John had bought in Seattle when the old car had balked and shuddered to a stop on the way to Lake Louise.

"You will note the identical tread," Don Sexton said, showing her the matching casts of the tread marks.

She nodded.

"No road scars, no small flaws on either set. Doesn't that strike you as unusual?"

"No," she said. "It only strikes me that whoever drove that car had just bought an unflawed set of new tires, as John and I had."

"That doesn't seem to be overly coincidental to you?" he asked.

She shook her head. "Maybe their tires were bald, too."

Then he became angry. "You don't seem to realize, Mrs. Hastings" (He always called her Mrs. Hastings because he knew it annoyed her. That was childish, too, she decided.) "That we intend to find the murderer of Graham Hastings, no matter who it is."

"I hope you do," she said, meeting his eyes. He moved away fretfully.

But her disorientation grew. Her serene house had become tensely watchful. The face in her mirror was a furtive face, darkened by the suspicions of others.

But most of all Sydney grieved at the change in the nature of time. The very stuff of her life, once so smoothly flowing, had slowed to a stop, gathering into eyeless pools of hours that must be bridged by conscious acts.

She exaggerated Wagner's needs, walking him oftener and oftener along his wild private trails. She tidied things, a job she had always loathed. Strangely, after her drawers were immaculate, she discovered that disorder itself had been suggestive of life.

Her gloves were all in their satin case for the first time since John gave it to her. Her jewelry was even sorted by colors of stones. Still there was time.

She finished the needlepoint pillow top she had been making. Then she folded it and put it away.

"Aren't you going to block this?" Lena asked when she found it on the linen closet shelf.

Sydney shrugged. "I hadn't thought about it."

Lena pulled it out with her hand and studied it.

"It's awful pretty," she said. "You done a nice job."

"Would you like it, Lena?" Sydney asked. "I was only

doing it. I didn't really want it at all."

"Are you sure?" Lena asked, holding the work nearer her, coveting, warring with her fear that Sydney might think she was hinting for it.

"I'm really sure," Sydney told her. How could Lena think that square of worked canvas mattered?

"If you're *really* sure." Lena's eyes brightened. Sydney could see Lena planning the backing and where the zipper should go.

"I'd like you to have it," Sydney said, "more than anyone."

In a sudden burst of self-denial, Lena folded the canvas and set it resolutely back on the shelf. "I can't. It wouldn't be right."

Then she moistened her lips and said, "Not with Lars and all."

"What has Lars got to do with your accepting a silly pillow top?" Sydney asked.

"He's on me about working for you," Lena blurted out. "He wants me to quit."

Lena couldn't face Sydney. She stretched for the next shelf of the closet, straightening the stacks of sheets so their edges were as precise as reams of paper. Her hands moved swiftly on to the towels.

Sydney felt cross. "For heaven's sake, stop fiddling with that stuff and tell me what's gotten into Lars."

"He thinks the children need me."

"But they're in school all day," Sydney protested. "You told me that yourself. And what about the money you are saving to buy a ranch?"

Lena's face brightened. "Money's easier now," she said happily. "Him and Bill and another guy are in some deal together. He says the money for the ranch is no matter for me to fret for—not anymore."

Sydney fell silent. Panic struck her that Lena might leave her. Sydney saw her days crumble into shapeless hours alone with Wagner.

With her hands bidden to stillness, Lena's restlessness moved to her feet. She shuffled in place like a child.

"Oh, come on, Lena," Sydney coaxed. "Relax. I don't eat people, you know. Tell me what's gotten into that big dumb Lars."

Lena grinned tentatively. "He just acts dumb," she corrected. "He's smart as all get out really. He only acts dumb because it's his way."

"I was only kidding," Sydney recanted, "Tell me why he wants you to quit."

"There's the talk," she said reluctantly.

"What kind of talk?" Sydney asked.

"About you and Mr. Fast," Lena said, her hands moving again, this time plucking at the cording on the back of the chair.

"What kind of talk?" Sydney asked again. Something cold and painful formed in her chest.

"Questions. They ask me questions. Like did you two fight? Did Mr. Fast have another woman somewhere? I told them 'no' quick as anything," she declared defensively. 'Whatever for?' I asked, 'with her pretty like that, all blonde and always half smiling?' But they ask."

"But that's not talk, Lena," Sydney corrected her. "Those are questions. It's dirty and ugly and demeaning, but that's the only way the police know to find out why John was killed."

Lena still looked away. "There's other talk, too. People in town," she paused, "thinking maybe you had a boy friend . . . being so much younger than him and all."

34

"Nasty backstreet rumor-mongering," Sydney said angrily. "You know better, and Lars must, too. That shouldn't make you quit a good job!"

"And it gives me prickles to know they are always watching."

"Who's watching?"

"Them." Lena waved her head toward the hill. "Those men. They watch this place day and night. Lars sees them coming and going. Even at night. Like buzzards they are."

Sydney frowned. Police surveillance would explain Wagner's fretfulness, his nocturnal alarms. "For God's sake, why?" she asked pettishly. "What do they expect to see?"

"Who understands cops?" Lena said. "Like why do they keep trying to get things out of me?"

The bastards, Sydney thought angrily. Running around behind my back, persecuting Lena and her family.

"They want to make out there was something strange about the two of you. I tell them, 'No!' You were just like that—'loners.' I told them."

"They're just trying to find out who killed John," Sydney decided aloud. "It's their job."

"Yes'm, I guess so." Her tone was less than convinced. "But Lars don't like it."

"I don't like it either," Sydney said. "You can tell Lars that. But tell him I need you. Tell him they'll get tired and go away and forget. People always do, you know. They get tired and go away."

"Maybe he'll listen," Lena said doubtfully.

"*Make* him listen," Sydney coaxed. "For me. And please take that pillow top, Lena. I want you to have it."

Lena took the pillow and went away. But another fragment of peace was gone from her house. The climbing
moon was a threat over the hill that night as she walked
Wagner. The stirring of the leaves was not wind but a
presence.

She buried her hands in the warm folds of Wagner's
neck.

"They think I killed John," she told him. "They don't
understand that whoever killed John killed me, too."

Wagner whimpered to remind her that he was capable
of pain.

"There isn't any Sydney Fast without John," she explained to Wagner. "If I killed John, I would be killing
myself."

Then she thought how easy it would be. The sea was
there with its careless bounty of violence. Even if she
feared falling, a small path went down, past rock and
through mesquite—the path Wagner liked so well. She
needed only to begin to walk. "I could tell myself I was
walking to the sun's end," she told Wagner. "Into the
sunset forever, out of the dark."

7

When John had been there, they ate in different places. He liked sandwiches on the deck on still days, or a bouillabaisse by the fire when fog lay against the windows. The round table was for morning and the square one for night.

Now the table was always the same. One place mat, one napkin, and silver in a polished line.

A chill came over Sydney when she heard Lena setting that table.

Sydney had always done her own cooking. Even when they travelled they got accommodations with a rudimentary kitchen so she could putter about with breakfast and lunch. She liked everything about food, prowling markets for perfect heads of romaine. She liked the feel of a knife against the crisp flesh of vegetables. She liked simmering complex sauces slowly to excellence.

All that pleasure disappeared into her torpor. Lena, noticing, added an evening meal to her day's work. It was a thoughtful gesture, but gratitude didn't make the food palatable to Sydney.

After Lena left, Sydney would smear her plate with food and rinse it indifferently so that Lena would know the plate had been used. Then the rest of the meal would go gargling and chomping into the garbage disposer.

Only Wagner ate, his hips wagging satisfaction as food plummeted into his swelling stomach. That was all right. Wagner was used to eating alone.

The Tuesday that would have been John's birthday came sunless under a sultry sky. Sydney was grateful to be taken in for more questioning. Their impatience—anything—was preferable to the silence of her house. Other birthdays materialized in that silence, days of sun and early snow, rooms once visited whose candles still wavered in her mind.

"Once past this day," she told herself, "I shall begin to heal. They will give up and go away. After two weeks, they must realize . . . they must know that they are wrong about me."

That night the fog was heavy. Although Sydney lit the fire that Lena always laid, it only made her more restless. Fires are for sharing, like food, she decided, taking her glass of white wine upstairs.

The fog was so dense that the railing of her bedroom deck was only an obscure line of darkness.

They can't watch me tonight, she thought smugly. They'll chill in their watching places and be miserable, and I don't even give a damn.

Cheered by the privacy of the fog she undressed and gave up the day.

In her nest of cushions she discarded amusements one by one. The words of her book were too frail to engage her thoughts. For a time she let the television screen flicker greenly without sound, but the creatures who peopled that curved space were jerky and plastic, with their mouths too wide in talk and their gestures too schooled.

She fell asleep with mingled relief and dread, knowing that early sleep invited the dream she was fearful of having.

Wagner wakened her. He came to her bed, whimpering. When she stroked his head drowsily, his whine became more pleading.

She decided no one was there. If someone were there, he would be barking frantically, hurling himself against the door. When she sat up he ran to the door, as if begging. Then she remembered. In her self-absorption she had neglected his night walk. The poor fellow hadn't been out since late afternoon.

"Just a minute," she told him, shrugging into a sweater and slacks. He watched from the door, his ears stiffened by her promise.

Once on a flight she and John had stopped in an airport at Reykjavik. The shops held mingled junk and marvelous handicrafts. It was so beastly cold that she shivered in the light suit she was wearing.

John found the fur-lined leather coat with swirling embroidery along the front and about the hem. It weighed a ton. When he wrapped her in it she felt warmer than she could believe.

"How is it in there?" He had grinned, peering at her with the fur collar turned up.

"Like the inside of a reindeer," she told him.

"We'll take it," he told the girl, counting out money even as they paged the plane.

"I may never come out," she warned him.

He caught her elbow, starting for the plane.

39

"It's all right," he whispered. "I intend to come in and join you."

Leaving the windows open to the fog and the sea, she tugged the coat from the closet. Wagner danced back and forth as she struggled into the coat.

"We'll walk in the fog," she told him. "A good walk. Then we'll both sleep better."

Wagner was giddy with pleasure at the approval in her tone.

She brought the leash in her hand but didn't put it on him. He only chased deer and he would see no deer in that deep fog.

The sea thundered beneath the slope. If any pale moon rode above the mists, it was secret to her.

With her hand on Wagner's neck she paused outside the door. The purity of the fog held her immobile. She thought of the recurrent dream. Being in the night fog was like her dream transformed, as a picture changed by the trick of developing. Instead of the harsh light of the dream, there was the envelopment of the fog, a paleness wrapping her body as thoroughly as the merciless light always did.

And like the dream, there was no shadow here. She felt her body losing its substance, becoming one with the fog and the stirring of the wind.

But the horror of the dream was not there. She puzzled over this difference. She was gone into that clinging paleness, but the loss of Sydney Fast was somehow not important because the burden of her guilt disappeared, too, leaving her clean and utterly free. In her exhilaration she started running toward the steps to the beach.

The pathway to the beach was perilous in any season. Stones had been hacked into primitive stairs by a warm-faced Spaniard John had hired. It took so long that when he was through, she missed that chipping sound rising through the sea's voice.

She set her feet carefully on the wet steps, gripping the shrubs that clung to the cliff side.

Every few steps Wagner stopped, looking back for fear she might renege on her promise.

When they reached the rocky beach, Wagner took off at a gallop, searching and hunting among the pillared stones.

The tide was going out, leaving the rim of beach bubbling with life. The level line of the sea, even in the dark, held inner curling lights. Some foolishness deluded Wagner that they were not alone. He ran to her side, then turned to bark fiercely into the jagged rocks that climbed the cliff side.

"Don't be silly," she rebuked him, staring through darkness at the wet stones.

The random whimsy of the fog gave the stones life. She watched them intently before turning away, determined not to be spooked by tricks of light or the hysteria of an overcautious animal.

Wagner's barking faded as he raced away to explore among the threatening rocks. She turned again toward the sea, telling herself what she must do.

Sydney was distracted by a sudden stillness. Wagner, having satisfied both his needs and his curiosities, had fallen silent. She turned and called to him, shouting into the fog.

When no answer came, she walked toward the stones, heedless that her boots sank deeply into the wet sand, filling with icy water.

She tried to whistle that high strong call that had been

John's way of bringing Wagner back. The whistle that she managed was weak and ineffectual as always. The sound of John's laughter at her efforts echoed faintly in her mind.

She was all the way to the pillar of rocks when she saw Wagner. At first her mind would not accept what she saw. She knelt down to where he lay in a pool of trapped water between giant stones. He was moving on his side as if restless but his eyes were open and staring. As she watched, the sea caught the carcass of the dog and pulled it from his small house into the larger room of the stirring sea. She reached for him, but as he slipped away she felt the smoothness of his flesh, only a little cooler than life. The great open wound in his head was feeding the gray gentleness of his mind into the circling water.

Her scream tore through her throat, becoming a sudden sharp agony in her lungs. Then the sea was suddenly all around her, flinging salt in her face, adding to the heaviness of her own body falling.

What had begun as a second scream died in the darkness of her fall.

From out of the darkness came a sound that she could not at once find meaning for. Muttered curses were broken by grunts and labored breathing. She tried to twist away from whatever dragged her body roughly across the stony beach.

The coldness in her bones and the green retching that thrust upward from the depth of her stomach arched her body with pain. She could not open her eyes to see Wagner again staring sightlessly into the curling water. She was sick and tired and chilled past a wish for life. But the voice was harsh and demanding.

"All right," it said fiercely, "get it together."

She opened her eyes with painful effort before shutting them quickly. It appeared to be Don Sexton, grown old and tired and white with fury.

"Wagner," she said. "Somebody killed Wagner."

He didn't acknowledge her words. He only pulled at her roughly. "Move!" he shouted.

When she hesitated, he shoved angrily. "Move, I say."

She began to cry again, but Don Sexton was ruthless. Supporting her with his arm, he forced her leaden feet to walk. Shivering and weeping, she mounted the stairs as he thrust her forward.

Sometimes they stopped a long time for her to rest, and sometimes he dragged her reluctantly over the hard places.

He pushed open her front door and led her straight to the kitchen where he tugged her coat off onto the gleaming floor. Sea grapes clung to the fur and a greenish bracken slid in the water on the floor.

She stared at it. John had been like that. But John was dead.

She shivered there in the kitchen, staring at the clothes on the floor. She must hold them in her mind, examine them carefully, search the lines again and again, anything to block from her mind the memory of Wagner and the tug of the sea stirring his lifelessness.

But Sexton was officious, barking her upstairs to shower and change. She obeyed him, even though the heat of the shower only drove the coldness deeper into her bones.

When she returned he was staring morosely at the freshly lit fire with a neat glass of Scotch in his hand.

He filled a snifter half full of brandy from the bar and cradled it only a moment in his hand.

43

"Okay," he said, thrusting it at her. "Down the hatch."

She coughed at the first swallow, then, meeting his eyes, drank again. A broad fan of flame spread through her chest. Her throat felt burned shut.

"Now sit down."

"You're wet," she said when her breath came back.

"So have new slip covers made," he said.

"I meant you should change," she said.

He shook his head. "Now tell me why you did that," he commanded. "It was *his* dog, I guess."

She stared at him incredulously. His voice was distorted with disgust and loathing. Back of his tone lay those endless hours of questioning, his devious efforts to create a guilt for her woven of his own fantasy. It was as if she were seeing him and herself clearly for the first time. He was a small power in need of a victim, and she had been selected. By that curious alchemy that is human morality, she had, as victim, become something loathsome and reprehensible.

A slow fire began inside her, a pure blaze of anger that burned away her torpor and her docility. Shock, hell, she raged inwardly. I have copped out, that's all. The fools, I have been patronized and brutalized by fools!

Her words came out sharply. "You think I killed Wagner?" She was giving him a chance, she told herself furiously. This is your last chance, Don Sexton, to take some other cover than that of a fool.

"Oh, come on, Mrs. Hastings," he said, smiling wryly.

His smile was the end. She was on her feet, her fists tight against her hips.

"You fool!" she shouted. "You ignorant blundering fool! Why in the name of God would I kill the only living thing I have left in my life? My God, how have you survived with such limitless stupidity?"

Incredibly, he stayed calm. His words were drawn out slowly, as if with patience for a child's understanding.

"Did you see anyone else on the beach?" he asked.

"I didn't," she flared, "but Wagner did. He wakened me and led me right down there. He went for the rocks and I, like a ninny, thought he was just imagining things."

"So your story is that someone was waiting there and overpowered that two hundred pound dog?"

"I haven't got a story," she said. "Wagner wakened me, wanting out. I took him. And now Wagner is dead. I found him there, with his head ... the way he was." Her words trailed off in a sickness of remembering.

"And why do you think someone was there? For what reason? Any quick-witted theories about that?"

"Jesus," she breathed, staring at him. "This is not my season for understanding. Why was my husband living under a false name? Why was he run off that cliff? Why do you insist on circling me like a patient vulture? As a matter of fact, how come *you* were there? Maybe it was you that Wagner was after? Sneaking around my house, snuffling for guilt."

He shook his head. "Now come on," he said. "Sure, we have kept a watch on the house. The lights went out early and then came back on about midnight. You were seen creeping out into the fog, does that make any kind of sense?"

"Wagner came and wakened me," she repeated. "He came and wakened me."

"So instead of walking him on the usual path you go to the beach," he said.

She shook her head. "He didn't have a leash on. I

followed where he went. It isn't the first time," she added defensively.

He nodded. "But in a fog like this?"

She stared at him, feeling his words weighing against her, adding to the enormity of the guilt he had manufactured for her.

"I was in the carport," his voice prodded. "We stay close during fog. I heard you scream. What if I had not been there? What would your story have been?"

She shook her head, "I don't have a story. I've never had a story. I didn't kill Wagner. I didn't kill John Fast." Now she was shouting, almost incoherently.

Don Sexton rose, his face flushed with his effort for self-control.

"Then, by God, you need a lawyer worse than anybody I've ever seen." His voice came brittle and low. "One thing had us stumped. We couldn't figure out how that car of yours got back in the carport that morning. There's not a turnaround for miles, and there was hardly time."

She stared at him, waiting.

"We finally found your tire marks," he said. "Our casts are plain. And there were paint chips from your car on a mazanita by the road. It was a mean piece of driving and dangerous as hell on this road, but we found where you turned the car, a mile and a half down—a U-turn in the middle of the road, a little jockeying, and back north to home."

"I didn't kill John Fast," she shouted again.

"Then you better, b'God, find a spellbinder to make a jury believe that."

She stared at Don Sexton. The house was still. John was gone. Wagner was gone. Only the pulse of the clock in the hall acknowledged time. But time, like the surf, was sweeping her nearer to the judgment in Don Sexton's face.

For the first time since John had died she was seeing a human being whole. Don Sexton was alive and firm and wary as he returned her gaze. Her own body tingled with aliveness. The torpor that had turned to fury at Wagner's death was supplanted by terror.

She shook her head to disperse the last shreds of the fog that had encased her, weighing her down. When she first tried to speak, the words couldn't come. After moistening her lips, she tried again.

"Help me," she said finally into the silence of the empty house. And then, from the reflexes of her years of docility, she corrected herself. "Please help me," she whispered.

8

While the clock in the hall stopped time, Don Sexton stared at her. She watched his expression change to incredulity.

"You're serious," he decided aloud, his voice rising with disbelief.

She nodded, not trusting herself with words.

He rose to move restlessly across the room. With new Scotch in his glass, he returned to her, his face bland again. His voice was level again but warning. "It's damned hard to help someone you don't understand." He shrugged, "I've tried. I've told myself you were shocked beyond reaction and waited for that to pass. I told myself you were too shy to communicate. Failing in those, I admitted that if I understood you at all—and I don't say I'm right—that you, Sydney whoever-you-are, are the coldest-blooded creature, man or woman, that I've ever encountered."

Sydney waited.

"Look at this thing from my view," he almost pleaded. "A man has been killed. I never knew the man or saw him alive but all of a sudden he's my job. So what do I get from you, his wife? A name that he apparently made up, a past that you don't claim to know about, and a fuzzy faraway look if I ask you a direct question. I sometimes wonder if you even knew Graham Hastings."

"I knew John Fast," she corrected him.

"Well, I know Graham Hastings," he told her, perching himself awkwardly on the arm of the divan. "You want to know what I have scratched out about your John? Do you want to know about the Graham Hastings who was pushed off the cliff that foggy morning?"

"It was clear that morning," she corrected him. "Clear and bright."

"By the time you and I got there it was, but the Italian fishermen said they saw the body falling through fog. Okay to give me that?" His voice rose with anger.

She shrugged. "I give you early fog," she agreed.

"See? There you go again," he said. "I offer to tell you the background we've dug up on your husband and what do you do? You play word games. Can't you ever push the words aside and look at it like it is . . . or don't you dare?"

"John had nothing to hide," she said recklessly. Don Sexton stared at her, waiting. Because John had looked at her that way sometimes, she knew what Don Sexton was doing. He was waiting for her own words to echo in her ears, for her to hear what she had said and realize that she wasn't playing the game straight. What did she have to gain by hiding from the truth about Graham Hastings? What did she have to lose?

"I'm sorry," she said.

He spread his hands out and stared at them as if the results of his investigation were written out there between them on invisible sheets.

"Graham Hastings was the son of Spencer Hastings

49

and Dominique Leclerc. He was born in Atlanta, Georgia, where his grandfather owned a prosperous bank. There is no record of his schooling in Georgia. His father died at the ripe old age of thirty-three with cirrhosis of the liver. The next trail we found were records of his having been expelled from two private schools in the midwest."

He stopped and stared at her. "Any of this ringing bells?"

"No," she said frankly. "Go on."

"Right after he left the last school, he nearly blew it in Chicago when he was eighteen. He had received a draft notice, but hadn't reported. He was accused of murdering a young girl in a near North Side flat. He was cleared of that murder because of insufficient evidence."

He stopped and waited.

"So he didn't do it," she reminded him.

"That murder is still unsolved," he pointed out. "But something seems to have changed the kid anyway. He got his draft call, entered the service, and had an exemplary four-year record. He came home with an honorable discharge and a Purple Heart."

She nodded. "That was the scar—a jagged red scar on the right side of his chest."

She waited, but he only sat quietly, watching her.

"Go on," she finally said.

"That's all."

"That's crazy," she said. "It can't just end there."

"You tell me," he suggested.

"I don't even know what time we're talking about," she said frankly.

"According to his records, Graham Hastings was honorably discharged in the fall of 1945."

She shook her head. "I can't help you very much for a long time."

"Try," he challenged her.

"My God! How can I try to reconstruct somebody else's life before I was born?"

"Where?"

"Iowa."

"Is that where you met John Fast?"

She shook herhead. "That was a long time later."

"Tell me about it."

Her brandy was gone and he refilled her glass without asking. She swirled the amber liquid in the glass, staring at it.

He frowned and said, "Can I just ask you?"

She nodded.

"You lived in Iowa, with parents?"

She nodded again.

"High school?"

"With honors," she said wryly, remembering the agony of graduation, her parents' pride, and a bilious green dress that rustled when she walked.

"Then college?"

"University," she said. "Iowa City."

"But you didn't meet John there?"

She shook her head. "I graduated from there in 1970."

"Took you a while," he commented.

"I changed majors a lot—twice, I think."

Funny thing, she had liked all the majors she had tried. It was just that whenever she saw the end growing near, she grew afraid. Her counsellor had finally grown pettish about it that last year. This same counsellor had opened the next door to her, suggesting that she apply for a scholarship for graduate study.

Sydney caught Sexton's eye on her, his impatient, speculative eye.

"I was thinking about that," she explained. "How I happened to go on."

"Graduate study?"

She nodded. "I just began graduate school when I ran into John. He had the newest doctorate around and had just made associate in the English Department."

"There's still a long time to be accounted for," he said thoughtfully.

She nodded. "He had to have been in school a lot of that time. Maybe nine, ten years."

"Why do you say that?"

"He hadn't been a student before the war, if what you say is true. It takes time to get a doctorate."

He nodded, absorbing her logic.

"So you went together . . . a long time?"

"It wasn't like that," she told him. "I worked in the library, part of my scholarship arrangement, and he spent a lot of time there. Pretty soon we were together a lot." Her voice wandered off. There wasn't any reason to go into how flattering his attention was, how one arrangement had led to another.

He corrected himself. "So you were together a lot for a long time and then you were married?"

She flushed. "That was it. In 1971."

"And you went to school and he taught?"

She shook her head. "We were sort of cashiered out," she admitted with a what-the-hell feeling. "Student living in sin with a member of the staff."

"And John?"

"He said he was tired of teaching anyway. After that we travelled."

"Didn't you think it was curious to be able to quit work and just wander around? Didn't you wonder where all the money came from?"

She shrugged. "He mumbled about investments. He didn't worry, so I didn't."

Sexton was studying her cautiously. "So you were married to this man for seven years. Did you understand him?"

"I could please him," she countered.

"But did you understand him?" he pressed.

"He was a secret person."

"Go ahead," he said. "Fly away into fuzzy words again. We're all secret people. There's no other way to live. You stalk about in your damned cool mask and inside there is something else, something you're hiding. I have a different mask, tougher maybe, not so polished, but I lived in mine too. It's the only way we can survive, you and I and the rest of them . . . by agreeing to this mutual secrecy."

"It doesn't seem decent or fair to strip off John's mask when he's gone."

"Was your husband through?" he asked. "Had he jogged all the mornings he wanted to? Had you two spent all the hours you wanted together? Was death a thing he would have chosen?"

"God, no."

"Then he was robbed," he said, jamming his hands deeper into his pockets. "Somewhere in those missing years is the answer to who killed Graham Hastings. That is, if you didn't do it."

He looked different when he was angry, larger somehow, and more vulnerable. What made this man angry over the death of John Fast? Sydney looked at the fine pressure of his cheekbones against his flesh, the hollow-ness of his skull where his dark eyes moved. Perhaps John reminded him too much of his own mortality.

He glanced at his watch and rose. "I'm due to report in," he explained.

Then at the door, "That didn't help much, did it?" he asked.

"It's a start," she said.

She shivered as she carried the glasses into Lena's immaculate kitchen. She felt that the chill of her alone-ness, like the chill from the sea, would live in her bones forever.

But her own terror at the guilt that Don Sexton was pressing upon her would one day bear her away.

John and she had shared the same closet. The architect had wanted to build two separate closets in the wall of the master bedroom, but John had protested. "Make it the length of the wall, if you want to," he said firmly, "but we want to share a closet."

She had said nothing but had smiled. John liked the fugitive scent of her perfume, which clung to his suits. He was entertained by the color of their clothes stirred in together like a haphazard pudding, his dark among the apricots and pale blues of her own things.

At the end of the closet shelf, under a pile of heavy-weather sweaters, was a gray box with its key taped to the bottom.

She opened the box and spread its contents out on the bed. She shivered as she sorted the contents into piles. There were insurance policies in neat plastic jackets, a long brown envelope marked "Will and Trust," then the deed to their house, which she had seen when they had built it. At the bottom was another long sealed manila envelope marked *Personal* in large block-shaped letters underlined three times.

She glanced at the door, remembering. ✄

It had been the year she had turned thirteen. Strange agonies of maturing had tugged at the child in her, reducing it to instant hot tears. People she knew well became strangers over a month, and the unevenest sort of anguish came suddenly at the turn of a moon or the angle of a hill.

She had returned to her bedroom to find her mother perched on the bed reading her journal.

Her mother had closed the book, laying it aside. She had put an arm around Sydney's stiffness. "How fast my little girl is growing up," she said. "A mother's God-given responsibility is to watch over a child, Sydney. You do understand that?"

Sydney had nodded assent while her throat ached with silent rebellion. After some gentle platitudes, her mother had left.

When her mother's footsteps died away, Sydney had torn the pages of that diary into fragments that fluttered like green-lined snow about her room.

She had never kept a journal again.

Sydney laid the envelope marked "Personal" aside.

There were three insurance policies. She was the beneficiary of each of them. With cool shock she saw that they were signed "Graham Hastings," although they were all payable to Sydney Jenkins Fast.

The envelope marked "Will and Trust" held only a letter and a memo sheet. The letter was to Graham Hastings, informing him that the attorney whose letterhead adorned the sheet was privileged to handle the affairs of his estate, and that his documents with securities had arrived and were on deposit with the trust officer.

She placed the insurance policies and the letter from the attorney on her dresser. One by one she replaced the envelopes in the box. When she came to the envelope marked "Personal," she held it again for a guilty moment. Then she fitted it into the drawer of John's desk along with his other special things she had put there: his favorite pipe, a pair of pocket binoculars he used for gull watching, and a single well-polished buckeye that he once told her had been to hell and back without changing color.

"R. O. Alexander," she repeated to herself as she lay waiting for sleep. She even persuaded herself that there was a warm and friendly sound to the syllables of that strange attorney's name.

9

During that long night, Sydney listened to the wind against her windows. The house itself belonged to time and silence. Only the deep pulse of the clock stirred inside the house.

Exhaustion had kept her from thinking clearly. Help. She needed help and now she had its name. She said the attorney's name aloud. "R. O. Alexander."

Impatience brought her from the bed. She could not rest until she began. She wrestled her bag from the storage room and folded her clothes into it.

Writing the note to Lena wasn't easy. She wrote, crossed out, and began again.

"Dear Lena," she wrote, "I have to make a quick trip to San Francisco to see John's attorney. If Mr. Sexton calls, tell him where I am.

"Wagner is gone. That is all I can say now. Please keep the house as usual. I'll be in touch. My best, Sydney Fast."

Dawn striped the sky above the airport in Monterey. There was even time for coffee and a sticky Danish before she boarded the Air West flight to San Francisco.

Not until a little after nine was she able to elicit a

response at R. O. Alexander's phone. Even then the answering voice was thick with morning.

"Without an appointment, I'm afraid . . ." the voice said firmly.

"But this is urgent," Sydney pressed. "I don't need a great deal of time . . . only a minute. Perhaps between appointments?"

"Your name again?" the girl asked.

"Sydney Fast," Sydney said, then added, "in reference to the estate of Graham Hastings."

"Hastings," the voice repeated without interest.

"I'll come in," Sydney said. "That way I'll be there when Mr. Alexander is free."

"But Mrs. Fast," the girl began.

Sydney replaced the phone, shutting the voice off. She couldn't afford the pressure of the girl's authority. R. O. Alexander was to be her friend. He had to be. He was all she had.

Sydney tried to divine what R. O. Alexander was like from his office. The room was a harmony of neutrals, creams moving into earthen brown, and finally the darkness of teak. An immense tree reached for the ceiling with filigree fingers. The secretary didn't count, Sydney decided. She was too carefully matched to the room. The cream of her hair, the leaf-green of her suit, the darker richness of her shoes. But the girl managed to convey disapproval in the air as she moved.

"Without an appointment." It was a delicate warning.

"I'll wait," Sydney insisted, feeling solid and planted and terribly gauche.

The room was too warm and music began. The selections irritated Sydney. Something childish and primitive in her wished for a malfunctioning window shade to snap in the quiet room, for a large ladder to creep down the secretary's hose. Instead people arrived, conferred, and were ushered out. Sydney battled her rising frustration at their ability to gain access where she was excluded.

The warmth finally lulled her to somnolence. At a little before ten the girl called her name with a hint of distaste.

R. O. Alexander was as self-conscious as his office décor. He stood to receive her, a tall fair man whose tan threw his blue eyes into sharp relief. He was turned out to be admired. Self-approval hung in the folds of his suit. A sapphire ring pained Sydney's fingers a little as he shook her hand.

"I'm Sydney Fast," she told him pointlessly, since the girl had announced her name as she entered.

"Please sit down, is it Miss or Mrs.?"

"Mrs. Sydney Fast." Then it struck her. "I know I have to be brief," her words tumbled out. "I was married to a man I knew as John Fast, Junior."

When she paused he waited, his face closed.

"He was killed . . ."—she paused—"two weeks ago yesterday. He was identified after death as being Graham Hastings."

He isn't helping me, Sydney realized with panic as he remained silent. He doesn't understand; he isn't helping me. But why?

She groped in her shoulder bag. The insurance policies in their neat slipcases, the letter marked "Will and Trust" slid across his desk to form an untidy heap. "This is why I came," she explained lamely.

He glanced at the documents without touching them.

"I have copies of those," he said. She felt hostility stir in the air. She groped for his sympathy.

"Did you know my husband was dead?"

59

He walked to the window so she could not see his face. "Not officially," he said. "I did get a message that Graham Hastings had been murdered." He paused before going on. "I was waiting some official word."

"May I ask what message this was?" Sydney asked.

"That doesn't seem germaine to our discussion," he said as if from a great distance.

For one terrified moment, Sydney thought she might cry. Instead she began talking quickly, almost incoherently. She spilled words at him, trying to reach some humanness warming the fibers of his silk suit.

"Mr. Alexander, I married my husband in good faith, under the name of John Fast, Junior. I never heard the name Graham Hastings until the police—"

"Have they found the murderer?" he interrupted, his eyes now full on her face.

He was like all the others. Questions, hostile eyes, challenge.

"I did not kill John Fast," she said.

"But I didn't say you did." His tone held triumph.

"They all think so," she said angrily. "They all do, and I have nowhere to turn, no one to help me."

"That's why you came here?" he asked. "I'm not a criminal lawyer, Mrs. Fast. That's not my field."

Only her fury saved her from becoming maudlin. She was grateful for her anger. This man was impervious to her anyway; anger at least gave her the power of her own words.

"Mr. Alexander." Her words came flat and clipped. She didn't care. She had come seeking an ally and found an enemy, damn him. He had chosen the roles, not she. "You were retained by my late husband as custodian of his will. You are the only link I have to the trustees of his

60

estate. If for some preconceived reason you have decided to behave in this cavalier manner towards me, it is
your own affair and not even interesting to me. I do
require—in fact, I demand that you either assume the
responsibilities inherent in your compact with my husband or refer me to someone capable of doing that,
preferably someone with the gift of common courtesy."

John's word cropping up there among her own, startled her to pause.

After a single look, R. O. Alexander's mask fell again.
His voice was milder. "Forgive any offense you have
imagined, Mrs. Fast. You are over-reacting. Also, please
remember you came without identification or appointment, following a most peculiar set of circumstances."

"Peculiar in what way?" she challenged him.

He shrugged. "In the first place I never met your late
husband. He was referred by a colleague with only the
comment that John Fast wanted his will checked to fulfil
the requirements of California state law and to have a
local attorney for the handling of his business. All our
business for five years has been conducted by mail. Now
suddenly there is a flurry of activity, once in July, again
in August, and then the message I mentioned and your
arrival. It is natural that I am wary of your sudden appearance."

His words echoed faintly in Sydney's mind. Her out-
burst had been followed by smothering fatigue. Wagner's death, the sleepless night just past, and the hasty
flight conspired against her. This sauve hateful man who
owned the droning voice swayed lazily before her eyes.
She could only see John—his back independent of his
desk chair, his long fingers tapping expertly on the little
Olympia in his study, a pale pillar of pipe smoke winding

its curved path towards the open window.

"What do you want?" she asked.

"Identification," he suggested.

The drill was somehow demeaning. Once there had been a roadhouse, a sleazy place bawdy with neon and huddled behind gas pumps and a miscellany of tired cars.

She and her escort could hardly see the bar from their table, the smoke was so thick. Broad-bellied men turned to peer at them. The owner wore a soiled apron with loose strings. Under his open shirt, an ascot of dark hair stopped at the stubble of his neck. He held her driver's permit to the light, checking for falsification. To feel that bare twenty-one again with palms sticky with sweat made her almost ill. She took her wallet back, unable to meet the attorney's eyes. She watched his ring wink with light as he folded his hands.

"I shall initiate legal steps to administer the will of Graham Hastings," he said. "I would not advise that you attempt collection on your husband's insurance policies until this matter of his violent death is settled. Do you have money?"

She nodded. "A checking account."

"With a reasonable balance?"

She nodded again.

"In the event that expenses need to be met, please contact me," he said. "As clearly as the will is stated, there should be no problem."

"I haven't seen the will," she reminded him.

He pushed a document across the table at her.

She shook her head. "What are its terms?" She was too strangely dizzy to cope with crisp sheets of legal language.

"You are the principal beneficiary," he said. "There are two small bequests: one to an orphanage in Michigan and one to a man in Chicago. The bulk of the estate is yours."

There was nothing to say. She thought of Don Sexton and the stream of facts he had poured out about Graham Hastings. Chicago . . . that made some kind of sense. But Michigan?

"If that is all, Mrs. Hastings," he said apologetically, "then you must realize that my schedule . . ."

As she rose, he was instantly behind her, catching at the collar of her coat.

"There's one thing more," she told him. "I need help."

"Would you like my recommendation for another attorney, one more specialized?" His question was delicate.

She shook her head. "You referred to a colleague—the man who sent John to you, I would like his name."

"But he's not here," Mr. Alexander said. "This was a long time ago."

"That doesn't matter," she said. "I want his name and his address—and his telephone number if that is available."

He shrugged before pressing a button on his desk.

"Mrs. Fast would like the address and phone number of Ted Cross in Phoenix, Arizona."

"I don't know what purpose this will serve," he told Sydney.

Just as suddenly as it had come, the dizziness began to clear. Sydney felt suddenly powerful. She smiled at him from the clarity of mind that had disappeared with John into the confusion of that morning so long ago.

63

"Someone killed John Fast," she explained. "Whoever did it has made every effort to implicate me. Somewhere in my husband's past is an enemy I don't know about. Maybe your colleague can help."

"I wouldn't pin too great a hope on that," he warned.

She folded the slip of paper the secretary handed her. You can pin hope on anything handy, she thought. There wasn't anything handier than that slip of paper.

Sydney fled to the airport to begin the jockeying of space and time that would bring her to Ted Cross.

The woman who answered Ted Cross's phone sounded professional and indolent.

"Mr. Cross is at tennis," she said smoothly. "He should be back about four."

"My name will mean nothing to him," Sydney confessed, "but please tell him that Mrs. John Fast, Junior, would like an appointment about five."

"Very well, Mrs. Fast." The voice was benign. "We'll hear from you again then, later?"

Like a nurse or a teacher, Sydney thought with irritation. Tennis at noon? From noon to four? She felt a stirring of interest in Ted Cross. Interest was safer than hope.

Walled in the telephone booth, she watched the crowds press by as the long ring sounded in her house on Big Sur. All her phones ringing into her known silent rooms depressed her. She hung up the receiver to dispel the somber image of that empty house.

Lena's number was easy enough to get. Among the legion of Jensen's in the valley, there was only one Lars.

At the third ring, a woman answered breathlessly.

"Lena?" Sydney asked.

"This is Pilar," the woman said. "Lena's gone."

Sydney hesitated. "This is Mrs. Fast, Pilar," she explained. "I couldn't reach her at the house—"

"Oh," the woman interrupted. "She's coming home for lunch."

Sydney checked her watch. "When do you expect her?"

"Any time," the voice replied. "But she might have stopped for cleaning supplies. Could I take your message?"

"That would be best," Sydney decided aloud. "Just tell her I am going to Phoenix before returning home. Tell her I'll see her early Friday morning."

"Want her to meet your plane?" the woman asked.

"Oh, no," Sydney said quickly. "Actually it's a late Thursday night flight."

"Lena wouldn't mind," Pilar suggested.

"That's awfully nice," Sydney said, startled at her own cordiality. "I'll just drive in."

Among the chorus of sounds, Sydney heard her flight called. Western Airlines via Los Angeles for Phoenix. She lost herself in the stream moving towards the boarding gate.

10

Deep lavender shadows lay on the mountains that walled Phoenix from the east. The traffic jerked dustily along palm-studded streets. John wouldn't have liked Phoenix, Sydney decided. He was restless in arid places.

She remembered Mesilla and the Billie the Kid bar. "Drink, drink to forget," he had said nervously, tapping a coin on the bar whose clear coating held entrapped silver dollars.

"It's beautiful," she had protested. "How can anyone hate the desert?"

"It's hard to run in sand," he said. She had laughed, but he had only drained his glass and motioned for another.

"The sky," she pointed out, "goes on forever."

He shook his head. "Not for me. Give me the green of spring thrusting from frozen ground, deep snows. It's probably all in what we got used to as a child."

As the endless blocks of Spanish houses flashed by, she found mystery in what had seemed like banter at the time. Hard to run in sand? What was John running from? What was hidden in the name Graham Hastings that made him fugitive? Not the murder charge—the detective Don Sexton had said he was cleared of that. And that bit about the world of his childhood. Georgia was no land of deep snows. She shook her head with confusion.

The woman with the indolent voice had a body to match, great flower-encased bosoms, and a wide smile beneath sunglasses.

"Mr. Cross is running late, but he said he'd be pool-side a little after five."

Sydney wound her way past sunbathers to a table. Multiple doors of apartments were separated from the highway by an expanse of crisp lawn.

She studied the complex. The emphasis was on convenience, with a restaurant and shopping mall right up the highway. Ted Cross lived easily and well.

When the glare from the pool forced her eyes shut, exhaustion closed in on her, She gripped the arms of the chair, willing herself to wakefulness.

Conscious that someone had approached, Sydney blinked herself awake. The slender man looking down at her was smaller than John. His skin was swarthy to the clipped line of his pale hair. Then this was Ted Cross, with his eyes too serious for the half smile on his face. His careful scrutiny produced a decision, for he caught her hands in his and said, "You must be Sydney."

"And you're Ted Cross," she said, collecting herself. "You're good to see me."

"My treat." He pulled a chair closer. "Look at the veiled curiosity, observe the side-of-the-mouth whispers. Can't you imagine what a furor you're causing? 'So that's who she was waiting for.' 'she could be his sister!' 'No way—not with a face like that.' 'Well, every dog deserves his day.' "

Sydney laughed.

67

"Let them whisper," he said happily. "It will make their day. Drink?"

"I've plunged about so much today that I'm not sure I'd stay together."

"The exterior is in good shape," he assured her. "Maybe something tall that you can nurse a long time. Gin and tonic?" he suggested.

He returned within minutes to set the tray on the table between them.

"Now seriously. You're John's widow."

She nodded, caught off guard by the unfamiliar phrase.

He stirred his drink lazily, giving her time. "Forgive me," he said finally. "I'm still in shock myself. I've had only an hour or two to get used to the loss of a friend." He paused. "Tell me about it."

To tell the story of John's death to someone who cared? The words wouldn't come. Instead the sun dazzled her into tongue-tied silence.

"Who are you?" she asked.

"John's friend."

"Why didn't I know?"

"We weren't that kind of friends."

After a moment he tried to help. "You were at Big Sur."

She nodded. "At the house John built there. On the cliff above the sea. On the lot John chose."

"And you've been there how long?"

"Five years," she replied.

"He wasn't doing anything . . . not teaching any more?"

"Not after we were married. He never taught after that."

"Reading a lot, walking, writing?"

She stared at him.

"You really want to know about our life?"

"I really do," he said after a minute, "but this isn't the time. For now, tell me what happened to John."

The words always came out the same. She wanted to vary them somehow, but she had been over that morning too many times. He listened intently, with only an occasional interruption.

"You had never heard that name Graham Hastings before?" he asked when she told him of the autopsy.

"Never."

"And that day, that long day that you slept. Is that usual for you?"

"Not at all," Sydney told him. "I guess I was trying to escape. I'm bad about things like that. I'm a coward really. I couldn't face the fact of his not coming back so I didn't."

"And since then there has been a steady interrogation?"

"Not steady," she tried to be fair. "Always they have some reason for asking new questions, something that has turned up."

"Tell me what they think is important."

"Mostly my car," she admitted. "They say my car ran John off. The tire tracks on the cliff are identical. There are paint chips from the underbrush down the road where the car made a U-turn. The tire tracks are there, too . . . on the shoulder."

He whistled softly. "I know that road. I wouldn't want to try that trick."

"I *wouldn't,*" Sydney told him.

"Then there's the money," she forced herself to go on.

"I never thought about money, I guess. That was John's concern. But apparently there's a lot of it."

"You haven't asked?"

"I guess I should have, but the only person was Alexander and I only saw him this morning."

"Anything else?"

"The thing is that they don't have anything," she cried suddenly. "They talk about the money and the difference in our ages. But the only thing they come to solid is the car. And I was asleep."

He nodded and frowned at the toe of his loafer.

"Tell me about the dog."

When she stared at him, he ducked his head.

"Goofed, didn't I? You hadn't told me about the dog."

A sudden chillness moved between herself and the back of the lawn chair.

He reached over and caught her hand.

"Look, Sydney, I got two calls today. One from you and one from Ralph Alexander. He told me a garbled tale about you. What would you have done?"

"I don't know," she confessed.

"Remember, one of my oldest friends has been murdered. I talked to the police at Big Sur, to a man named Don Sexton."

"So you wanted my story, too—to see if it checked?" Resentment hardened her voice.

"I need all the stories," he said calmly.

Sydney lifted her half-empty glass, then set it back down without drinking.

His tone was suddenly brisk. "I have a hazy idea of your day and it sounds exhausting. I have a plan that no sane woman would argue with."

"My sanity may need a good test," she admitted.

"Are you registered anywhere?"

"I didn't have time."

"Excellent. When the management has an open apartment, they make it available by the night . . . to guests with references. While you finish that drink, I'll check you in. Then you shower and sleep awhile. Then we can talk."

He checked his watch officiously. "Dinner will be at seven-thirty. My place." He winked broadly.

He stalled her protest with a raised hand.

"I like to cook . . . that's why I live like this. And that way we can talk."

She studied him, this sober-eyed man with the jesting tongue. She could see him as John's friend and her own. I am not alone, she thought with wonder. For the first time since John had left and not come back, she felt peaceful.

Then he laughed. "You're very transparent, Sydney Fast," he said. "I felt the measuring tape. Did I pass?"

She grinned and rose, downing the drink.

"You passed," she said. "Lead me to sleep."

She wouldn't have known that Ted Cross had been there while she showered except for the white roses on her dresser and the stout Scotch on her bedside table. A scrawled "DRINK ME" was fastened around the glass with a rubber band.

"Scotch and gin together?" she asked herself. The bed rolled lazily beneath her until the phone startled her awake.

"Charcoal's on." Ted's voice came cheerily. "I'll be there in half an hour to lead you in."

Ted's apartment was, Sydney decided, a triumph in conservation of space. Not one inch of space was wasted.

71

The table was crisply set with place mats and wine glasses and silver. A burgeoning cloud of fragrant smoke pillared from the patio off the kitchen.

"Not to be suggestive," he said, poking at them with a long-handled fork, "but they're New York strip."

"John was a porterhouse man," she told him.

"Some people never change." He sighed.

He swore as a sudden blaze engulfed the steaks.

"I'll administer first aid. There's salad, wine." He waved at the kitchen and bent over the broiler again.

Watching Sydney eat, Ted sighed. "How can you eat like that and be cadaverously thin?"

"I haven't learned to eat alone yet," she admitted. "I'm sorry," she added. "I don't mean to say things like that."

"Good God, girl, say anything you please. Remember, I'm John's friend."

"And mine?"

"I think so, Sydney Fast," he said. "Tell me why you came."

She stared at her wine glass, and he refilled it.

"Impulse," she admitted, "born of desperation. I don't like that Ralph Alexander."

"Why?"

"Maybe because he doesn't like me," she said. "He had his back up before he saw me. He was barely civil and not a little cruel. He's also a pompous ass who is drunk on himself."

Ted roared with laughter.

"It's good to hear that old friends have stayed the same."

"But you sent John to him," she said with amazement.

"I did and I would do it again. He was a student of mine. He is everything you said, but also impeccably honest and discreet beyond belief. Those happened to be the two qualities that John needed most in an attorney."

"Why those things?"

The coffee he brought was rich and thick and delicious. He set the brandy decanter beside the pot and lit a cigar.

"Honest, because a fortune was involved, and discreet because John wanted to be unavailable."

"But why?"

Ted studied her. "Surely you knew him as a solitary man, Sydney?"

"It was just his way," she began lamely. "He liked it best when there were just two of us. We never even had a dog until right there at the end."

"How close to the end?" he asked.

"Late August, early September—I can't really remember. John just came home with Wagner—out of the blue."

"Wagner," Ted said almost to himself. "Good Christ, couldn't I have guessed? You never guessed that John was running away . . . all the traveling, choosing that place, so secluded?"

"I just thought he didn't need more than just us. Am I awfully naive?"

"Not awfully, just charmingly, Sydney." His tone was rueful.

He tipped a half inch of brandy into her glass. "Alexander said you were trying to find someone in John's past to pin the murder on."

"That bastard!"

"Remember, Sydney, all he knows is what he reads in cryptic letters."

She stared at him, waiting for an explanation.

"Within days of John's death, Alexander got an anonymous letter accusing you of John's murder."

"Then that was the communication he was so enigmatical about?"

Ted nodded. "It upset Alexander, but I think it's pretty exciting. It adds an unknown to this cast of characters."

"I'm not sure I am following," Sydney admitted.

"Who else knew of John's death and your situation as the prime suspect? Who wished you ill enough to write to your attorney and accuse you of murder?"

Sydney shook her head. "Who?" she echoed.

"The other driver of Sydney Fast's red car," he suggested. "And for classical reasons, he should have been wearing red, be tastefully horned and exude a faint but unmistakable odor of sulphur."

11

He shouldn't do that to me, Sydney thought resentfully. He has no right to make an instant vision of hell stir in the charcoal ashes. The nightmare beyond faith yawned in the darkness of the trees.

"One of us has had too much brandy," she said.

"Oh, come now, Sydney," he said. "Who but the devil ever got John Faust? I'll accept a certain girlish naivete, but certainly the significance of that name didn't escape you. Dr. John Fast, Junior, indeed."

"I laughed about it." Sydney was defensive. "But I never knew he had another name." Then what he was saying struck her. "And anyway, you have to believe in God to accept the devil."

"Do you now?" He laughed. "I would say that you only have to know man."

"That's one conceit I don't have," she admitted. "I haven't known many men that well. My father . . ." She paused. "Tell me about John."

He stared at the coals winking in the hibachi. No wind stirred the formal line of trees, and only one star shone in the desert sky.

"First I just want to tell you how we met." He grinned

at her. "Knowing John like you did, it might amuse you.

"I was short of funds when I started college, and by the time I got to graduate school the shortage was critical. I had one of those schedules where you go from class to work and study half the night. I didn't mind that much except that I had always been somewhat of a jock. So I took up jogging."

He paused and Sydney grinned back.

"John and I were the same two solitary figures circling the campus in the gray of dawn for a month or two before we met. I was the one who started it, of course. I just hailed him one morning and suggested we have coffee.

"He looked at me the level way he did and asked 'Why?' I suggested that if our physical clocks went off at the same hour, we might have other things in common, too. To be honest, I was surprised when he agreed.

"It was fairly obvious that even though he had taught there several years, he didn't have any friends to speak of."

"He was a loner even then," Sydney mused.

"Worse than a loner. He was dour, walking around with the guilt of the world pressed on his eyebrows."

"Why?"

Ted shrugged again. "Who asks? But I taught him to play chess and drink. He didn't know how to play anything . . . even with words."

Ted hesitated and sighed. "This story is damned hard to tell. For so long I thought the whole thing was hilarious. I had a million laughs until I realized that John was playing it straight."

"What 'thing'?" Sydney asked desperately.

"This Faust bit," Ted said. "I couldn't believe it at first. When we started having Sunday breakfasts together

76

and then having a few beers those nights I wasn't tied up, there was one thing and one thing only this guy wanted to talk about, the Faust story . . . all the ramifications of selling your soul to the devil.

" 'I guess if your name had been Dracula, you'd have had a thing on with girl's throats,' I kidded him. He was rather deep into the cups that night and he smiled wickedly and said that I had just put the cart in front of the horse.

"He seemed to think that was pretty funny and went on to add that the compact with the devil had come first and the name later. I figured any man deserves a few wild statements after that much beer, so I let it pass.

"Then when I went to his place, there was this whole shelf of books about the Faust legend. It was eerie. He had every published version I had ever heard of—Goethe, Marlowe, you name it."

"So he liked Faust?"

"Not liked," he corrected her. "He was obsessed by Faust. I used to kid him about going to live in Wurtemburg, asked him to fix me up with Helen of Troy—stuff like that. Finally he did ease up enough that we talked about it."

"There's not that much to the story," Sydney objected.

"He thought there was. We'd talk about the force of the compact."

The word was an icy passage through Sydney's bones.

"He'd pose questions. If Faust had not consciously waited for the devil's return, would he have come? Did Faust, by knowing that hell was in the bargain, unconsciously seek hell?"

"But it wasn't that way at all," Sydney protested. "At

the last minute Faust pleaded for salvation, for himself and Margarete—at least according to Goethe."

Ted shook his head. "John maintained that the very act of fleeing—even to God—made Faust vulnerable to the devil's collection."

Sydney sighed. "What a burden to live with."

"That's the right word," Ted agreed. "And I think it was the size of the burden that finally brought him to tell me the whole story.

"He said that in the beginning he had been as nameless as a piece of cheese. 'I had a label,' he said, 'like a brand name stuck on for convenience in reference.' He had no sources or resources, no past and sure as hell no future. But he did have a hot-blooded immature friend who was rich beyond John's imagining. The friend was also what John called his 'spitting image.' The friend committed a 'crime of passion' which—if he'd been tried for it—would have resulted in a long term in prison, if not worse."

"What was the label he mentioned?"

"He never told me that. He only said that the Graham Hastings name carried a fortune with it, enough to give a man any future he chose."

"My God," Sydney exploded. "John wouldn't have done anything like that. He wasn't big on material things —not the John I knew."

"You have to remember this happened when they were teenagers. Your John was nameless and facing a hopeless future. Money looks pretty warming from that vantage point."

"But it's evil," Sydney protested. "The whole concept is evil."

"Back to Faust." Ted grinned at her. "That's where John made that mental leap. At the time it looked fair to him—he was possibly saving his friend's life and enriching his own. Later it looked evil."

"But couldn't John have given the money back?" she asked.

"He tried to." Ted said. "Graham apparently got into trouble and asked John for money. John sent it and tried to set up a meeting in the desert down by the border to straighten the whole thing out. His old friend set up an ambush and John barely escaped alive. That's when he changed his name. His 'Graham Hastings' label had become dangerous and he was eager to be free to be his own man. He chose the name John Fast, Junior, for the obvious reason. And lived under it for the rest of his life."

Sydney nodded. "And then?"

"Then he went back to school—straight through, got a job teaching, and you know the rest."

Sydney shook her head. "How do I know the rest?"

"I finished law school and went into practice. Finally I went into teaching myself, but we always kept in loose touch. He had used the same attorney all those years to manage his affairs. When he decided to settle down in California, he came and asked me for a man he could trust there. I chose Alexander. He said he was tired of running, that it was unfair to you, that he had decided to settle down and wait for the devil to find him in the classic manner of the legend."

"Then the devil who drove John off that hill must be the real and original Graham Hastings. I wonder if he still looks like John?" she asked miserably.

79

"The problem is how carefully John has covered his tracks all the way. Is there nothing? Nothing left there out of his past?"

"A file," Sydney admitted. "There was a file marked 'Personal' in his things."

"And what was in it?" Ted pressed.

"I didn't open it," she admitted.

Ted stared at her a moment, then laughed. "That's one for Guinness," he said.

"There are the bequests," she reminded him. "The man in Chicago, the orphanage, and then whatever is in the file."

He nodded, rising. "We'll run those leads out before we panic."

He saw her to her door. The lawn smelled green and artificial in the heavy air of night.

Then she remembered. "You laughed when I told you the dog's name was Wagner. Why did you do that?"

"Wagner was a student of Faust's, who would have protected him from damnation if he could."

She stared at him numbly.

"Marlowe called the student something else, but it was Marlowe's lines that Hastings always quoted.

> Were he a stranger and not allied to me,
> Yet would I pity him."

12

Sydney's room was bathed with an eerie filtered light from the blaze of sun filtering through turquoise-colored drapes. Inside that walled world a steady hum attested to the air conditioner's vigilance against the wave of heat that would be the Arizona day. The other sound, the one that came dimly into the room, was from another world, another time.

Bundled in the blanket pulled from her bed, Sydney parted the drape carefully like a prying child. A small man in a blue jump suit traversed the lawn slowly, his head concealed by an immense straw hat resting on the sunbaked brownness of his neck. As she watched, he swung the mower about, positioned it for a miniscule lap and, without breaking stride, plodded towards her, cutting a matching swath. Beyond, on the next stretch of lawn, the sprinkler heads were already swaying, catching, and turning again. On that patch of already sheared grass, great wide-legged bronze grackles stalked the beetles that floundered among the sodden roots.

It was already late. She could imagine Ted Cross up and off somewhere, showered and fed, bouncing about on his athletic legs to some errand of his own. A strange man. How little he had said of himself. Ted Cross, seen only in the context of his relationship to John Fast. But then, she had been the same. She pondered that long evening's talk, spanning the years of John Fast and this new insight into his mind.

In this filtered light of morning, Ted's story was confusing. She was astonished that never once in their years had John touched on this Faustian obsession.

Perhaps that too was normal. Did the original Faust explain the casket of jewels? She shook her head.

She needed to dress. Ted would come any time. She needed coffee, strong and black and maybe laced with sugar, to get her going.

She sat dejectedly in the small room that seemed to close in on her like a blue prison, a closed place where atmosphere recirculated endlessly like a refrain played over and over until the hearer broke into rebellious screams.

The day that John died. She played the day over again in her mind, letting it slip into the rhythm of the motor that stirred her air. When she wakened, had she heard a car sound? Would the car have been gone then? No. John would have missed it when he passed the carport. That was a point in time she had not snagged on before.

How long had she lain there between sleep and waking, listening to John's careful movements, to his colloquy with Wagner? Then she had taken the shower. Even wide awake she would not have heard the car being taken then. But the car had been waiting for some time. The marks at the roadside had established that much.

After that the minutes had gone too swiftly. What if the car had not been in the carport? Would John have come

82

back in to check with her about it? Or would he have run his allotted stint as usual?

He would have come back. She decided that firmly. He would have come back to stand at his desk with his hand loosely on Wagner's head to call someone . . . the police, someone. That is, unless he had lent the car to Lena. Sometimes he did that. Lena's old car was so undependable that John had finally given her a key to the Corvette.

With a sense of high excitement she reached for the phone. Ten o'clock in Phoenix—it would be nine at home. That would make it touch and go. Lena could be anywhere, even still at her own house.

She could be already at Big Sur or even in transit.

She abandoned the Big Sur number after six hollow rings. In her purse she found the memo pad with the number of the Jensen house in the valley.

Lars answered the phone on the second ring.

"Lars," she said, breathless with the excitement of her new theory. "This is Sydney Fast. Has Lena left already? I need to ask her something."

"She was stopping at the store on her way," Lars explained. He laughed softly. "She's determined to give that house of yours the best cleaning ever while you're gone and won't be bothered by her banging and thumping. Got some message for her?"

"Not really." Sydney hesitated. "After all, I'll be there when she gets in tomorrow morning. I was just wondering if by any chance she had used our car the night before." Sydney's voice failed suddenly. "The night before John disappeared."

A coolness was in his voice as he replied.

"I'll have to think back," he said slowly. Then he paused. "Maybe her friend, Pilar, might remember. She's just across the way if you want me to ask."

"Oh, never mind," Sydney said. "I'll just check with Lena in the morning."

"Yah, fine," he said. "Have a safe trip." His voice rose at the end like a question.

Lena's using the car would explain so much, she thought with sudden exhilaration. She might have left the key in it—in the glove compartment, as she sometimes did. Any chance passer-by . . .

She musn't let herself think about the devil that pursued John Fast. A chance passer-by would be so easy, so logical. And an accident, a genuine accident by a man driving a car he wasn't accustomed to.

But the car had been brought back.

She fled to the shower to escape the dark corners her mind kept driving her to.

Sydney was bursting to tell Ted her theory when he called, but his curious mood put her off. He stared morosely at the morning paper while she had coffee and a roll.

"Are you married?" she asked as he turned to the editorial page.

He glanced up, startled. "Good God, no."

"You must have been married sometime," she said. "Else how could you have developed such immaculate rudeness at table?"

He grinned sheepishly, laying the paper aside.

"Some of us come to boorishness naturally; others have to be trained. I am a natural."

"Never been married?" she asked, suddenly curious.

He shook his head. "Rather by accident really. It was

something I meant to get around to and didn't until it was too late."

"How do you know when it is too late?" She remembered herself in her twenties rationalizing her liaison with John Fast. It wasn't as if I were ever going to marry, she had told herself. It's my own damned business what I do with my body and my life.

He shrugged. "It was during one of my mother's visits to me. I really like the old girl. She's spunky and bright and independent and hilariously feminine. But after three days I got edgy. I liked being with her as much as always. It was more a matter of sharing air with another human all the time, having to interrupt my thoughts to make answers to questions that didn't provoke me. Having a book moved from where I left it. I knew I'd had it on cohabitation right then."

Sydney laughed. "That was an adjustment for John, too. For the first year or two he had the faintly strained look of a woman in an ill-fitting corset."

Ted laughed. "Maybe that's why he kept you travelling —to break his old patterns. I know that need to fracture molds when they begin to constrict you."

"Is this an old mold here, or a new one?" she asked.

He looked at her speculatively. "You ask good questions, Sydney Fast." Then he shrugged. "This is a transition for me. I have been teaching too long. I took a sabbatical, ostensibly for study. I am actually in the process of getting my head together to start a new life."

"Two of us," she said quietly. "If I come out of the first with any life left."

His face clouded at her words. He rose so abruptly that she left coffee still warm in her cup.

He insisted on taking her for a drive through the desert and then drove like a madman, barely replying to her in monosyllables. The place they had lunch was aflutter with solicitous waiters and so drowned in self-conscious classical music that conversation was impossible. Somehow the only exchange they managed to achieve was a heated argument about the necessity of anchovies in an Italian salad dressing.

Sydney's frustration mounted as the day waned. All this activity and his shrewd parrying of her questions had exhausted her. Ted fell into a long silence as he drove her to the airport, the hastily packed white bag bumping behind her bucket seat in his ancient TR3.

At the airport he turned off the key and sat, silently staring at the wheel. "Forgive me, Syd," he said, sounding contrite. "This was a bastard way to treat you, but I'm not a fast take. I needed to think things out today. To plan."

She wanted to lash at him, at the wasted hours, at the raised hopes of last night and his determined withdrawal of this day. Instead she waited, remembering John's warning to her when she had blown at him. "In the choice between biting off the other fellow's head or biting your own tongue, Syd, you better settle for your own blood. You have the unfortunate knack of memorable insult."

"Want to hear my plan?" he asked, still apologetic.

She nodded.

"They're after your scalp, Sydney. After talking to that Sexton character and Alexander this morning, I'm sure of that. You're on borrowed time now. Only the flimsiness of their circumstantial evidence has kept you out of the pokey this far. I have Sexton convinced that you are in firm legal hands—mine. What he doesn't know is that

I'm not being retained, I'm being involved.

"You go home as planned. Square things away there for a bit of an absence. Get out that personal file and open it, squeamishness be damned. I'll call you at midnight and be ready to record the lot. Unless there's a better lead in it, we start at the beginning."

"What is the beginning, Ted?" she asked.

He shrugged. "Atlanta, where young Graham Hastings began. Then there's Chicago, where the old murder happened. You remember, there's still a Chicago beneficiary in his will. That's our opening there. After that we'll play it by ear."

"Atlanta?" she asked.

"What could be more natural than the young widow visiting her husband's family?" he countered. "There could be nothing to learn there—or a great deal. We're fishing in pretty muddy water."

"And the orphanage in Michigan?" she asked, remembering Alexander's terse summary.

"That's a freebie we can dig into if we need it. I'll be in touch tonight. Remember to answer your phone at midnight and we'll make plans. Okay?"

"This is not fair to you, Ted," she said. "This isn't your fight. It's been a long time . . ."

He patted her knee, grinning. "Let's say that my slice serve is off and I'm bored without students to harass. Okay?"

He walked with her as far as security would permit, carrying the white bag.

"Not the least of my gratitude is that you can handle that Alexander popinjay for me from now on," Sydney confessed.

"Don't be too hard on Alexander, Syd," he said gently.

"He probably didn't tell you that John had taken out a new half-million dollar insurance policy late last summer. In your name."

Something chill swept through the air from the blue hills behind the town. She stood rooted to the ground.

Ted caught her hand and lifted it to his lips almost mockingly.

"Until midnight."

She nodded, then stumbled on the stairs, unable to see for a sudden mistiness of tears.

13

At ten seventeen the Hughes Air West plane eased to a stop on the runway at Monterey Airport. Sydney huddled in her seat in the half empty plane until the stewardess came with a questioning glance. Sydney smiled apology as she rose, still nursing her incredible exhaustion. Funny. She had gone full circle since leaving her little red car at this place. The high hope she had pinned to R. O. Alexander had been totally destroyed, only to be rekindled by Ted Cross's persuasive words in the clear bright sun of Phoenix.

But now even the memory of that hope seemed to diminish as she drew nearer Big Sur.

Night rain still stood in crystalline drops on the hood of the Corvette as she turned onto the highway south. She flipped on the radio only to turn it off a moment later in annoyance. Like the miles that slipped away behind her, she felt her self-confidence being spun off in the wet blackness of the night. The guilt was returning—she could feel it weighing down her arms on the wheel. She had lost the Sydney of the sanguine hopes somewhere between Ted Cross's last pressure on her hand and this place. All the things she couldn't bear to touch with her mind returned: the lazy memory of that last morning, Wagner's sensuous movement in the stirring tide, the eyes of her accusers telegraphing their determined belief in her guilt.

Not even her memories of Ted Cross's stubborn plan or her own marvelous theory about Lena and the car could fortify her against the growing depression. She was only conscious of her waiting house pressed steadily against its cliff by the unremitting wind, and of time running out with a policeman named Don Sexton.

She didn't like the games her mind played with her. The parody came to her without bidding and she could not rid herself of the singsong of the words:

> Her death that started with her birth
> At thirty-five befell
> They went to call the Sexton and
> The Sexton rang the bell.

Her mother's words, stern and terrifying in the ears of a child. "Mark me, Sydney, he who lives by the sword dies by the sword," then, sensing her child's confusion paraphrasing, "The anguish you visit on other people will come back to you a thousandfold."

Dreams of her childhood, that bright clear air that cast no shadows. The melting away of her body into waves of shimmer. Was this the anguish her mother had foreseen? Anguish, a thousandfold, blazing her into not being.

Her tires squealed in protest as she whipped into her carport and let the motor gasp to a throbbing stop.

The house lay in utter darkness. This was strange. John had carefully designed the wiring of the security lights. With a single silent switch the balanced lights came on, low but convincing, a pattern along the bottle glass windows of the upper hall, a closet at the other end of the house and deep in the living room, so that it cast only the faintest glow through drapes, a single round hanging globe. Lena had forgotten. That was simple enough—Lena had forgotten to turn on the security lights.

The emptiness of the house echoed her footsteps along the hall. Then at the touch of her hand the lights fanned all about her. Like mushrooms, the tables, chairs, and the clock in the hall sprang to their places from the anonymity of darkness.

Sydney walked from room to room like a curious child, staring at the immaculate order of the house. The floors caught the gleam of light in a patina of fresh wax, and the windows shone blue black, bearing not even the trace of the inevitable fog haze. Lars was right, Lena had outdone herself in cleaning.

Sydney flipped open the top drawer of the bar. My God. Even the coasters were in neat stacks by color, and the wine glasses on the shelf above glistened like a TV ad. But nothing stirred inside her. Nothing told her that this was home.

She noted the bowl of fresh lemons in the orderly kitchen. Lena had this thing about lemons. She picked them from her tree in season and brought them in a grocery bag complete with sprays of leaves. When her own tree was between seasons, she added them to the grocery list. Sydney could never decide what eventually became of those lemons. Did they disappear into drinks, into sauces or dressings? It didn't matter. To Lena a kitchen must have lemons, and the sharp freshness of their scent was somehow reassuring to Sydney.

Upstairs the wind pressed against her windows as she

undressed. The extraordinary tidiness of her closet astonished her. She fished among the plastic covers of newly cleaned clothes to find her robe.

She sat a long time at the dressing table, releasing and brushing her hair. "Things will be different now," she whispered to the woman in the mirror. "Things will be different and better than before." But the woman in the mirror looked back at her with level eyes, silent and unbelieving.

In some layer of Sydney's consciousness she registered the clock striking the hour. It must have been eleven. But the sound came dully through sleep. With a faint guilt she realized that she had not even missed its voice these days. Was this how it would be? Would all the things that had been hers and John's eventually leave her consciousness, gradually be made alien by her aloneness?

She was so deep in sleep that the pounding on the door was already a memory by the time it began again, along with shouting.

Groggy and disoriented, her heart thumping with terror, she made her way downstairs. She clutched her robe half about her shoulders, fighting the looseness of her hair about her face.

Beyond the chain the voices tempered as she stared out at them.

"Who is it?" she asked. "What do you want?"

Through the slit of the door she sorted them out: Lars, broad and ruddy in the half light of the porch, his great fists balled as if to strike. A fury seemed to contort his face and his eyes glittered a cold icy blue. And beside him Don Sexton.

"I don't understand," she said to Don Sexton, swinging the door wide.

"Lena," Lars shouted. "What you done with my Lena?"

"Lena." She shook her head. "She's not here. I only just got here."

They were barely inside before Lars plunged for the kitchen.

"What is all this?" she asked Don Sexton helplessly.

"This guy's frantic," Sexton explained, his eyes careful on her face as always. "Lena came here to work, he said, and never came home. He called her friends and everywhere she could have gone. He's convinced she's here. I finally gave in."

Lars' boots were heavy in her house. He was ranging through the hollow rooms like a desperate animal. "Lena! Lena!" The words caught on each other, tripping and re-echoing before he shouted again.

"She can't be here. I just got home and saw no one."

"And you've been through the house?"

She nodded. "I walked through when I got in; then I went to bed. There's no one."

Lars was back, his shoulders rounded. "Where is she? What have you done with her?"

"Lars," she protested. "I only just got home."

"Tomorrow," he said. "You was to come tomorrow."

"That's not right. I said I'd see her tomorrow." Her car, she thought suddenly. "Where's her car?"

"It's jimmied again, that's what," Lars said sullenly. "She was to call when she was through. But she never did."

"Maybe someone came along and gave her a lift," Sydney suggested.

93

"Way out here?" He was skeptical.

He turned away from them, opening doors and banging his way through the house again.

"When did you arrive?" Sexton asked.

"The nine forty-five out of San Francisco," she explained. "In Monterey a little after ten, and then I drove home and went to bed."

The clamor of Lars' progress ceased. Into that sudden silence the clock's voice sounded dolefully. Then there was that cry, a small hurt animal cry followed by a curse.

Instantly Don Sexton sped toward that sound.

Originally the room had been a large pantry, but even John was finally convinced it was unreasonably large for that function. The dividing wall was put in later. Louvres were built to the outside so that the angled air in that room was always cool. The sun never shone there, and along the wall the layers of wine bottles stayed always a little chill. The door must have been a stock size, but Lars seemed to fill it completely. Bare patches of light angled out from around his broad frame. He was shaking, the round heaviness of his back moving rhythmically in time with the racking sobs that filled the air.

"Here," Sexton said firmly, tugging at him, "What's up?"

The big man spun at the touch. His broad hands, bristling with whitish hair, were splayed across his face as the rhythmic sobbing grew louder.

Lena looked smaller than in life. Her dark eyes stared at them fixedly, her face frozen in an expression of bewildered astonishment. Her hair was back from her face and her position was unreal. She was curled like a child seeking reentry to a womb. One shoe was off and a wide webbing of run curved up her leg toward her calf.

94

Tightly around her neck, its ends at an elegant angle on her shoulder, Sydney saw her own pale apricot silk scarf, a gift from John.

Hypnotized by the horror in Lena's face, Sydney didn't see Lars turning towards her. Then she felt the pain of his blow, the sharp audible crack of her head striking the wall of the pantry as she recoiled from his hand.

"You," he shouted at her, starting towards her again, his eyes level with her own as he crouched with balled fists. "It's always you, ain't it? First that man you lived with and then his dog. Now Lena." Don Sexton was there, but could not stop the blow. Instead Sydney struggled fiercely as Sexton tried to restrain Lars.

"Murderer! Murderer!" Lars screamed as Sexton finally wrestled a gun from his pocket and backed him from the room.

Sydney didn't follow. She braced herself flat against the shelf feeling the shapes of cans and bottles pressed against her back. Pain still moved crazily along the side of her head. As she cringed against the wall the green waves of nausea came as they had before, with Wagner. Even with her eyes shut she saw Lena pressed against the insides of her lids, more visible than even in the naked light of that single hanging bulb. Lena, brightly scarved, curled on the damp floor of the wine cellar, her dark eyes wide and the single stockinged foot at that grotesque angle.

Don Sexton's voice was smooth with persuasion as Lars moved from fury to tears in diminishing storms. Then with sudden stridence the phone pealed in the kitchen beyond. Don Sexton reached for it, paused, and let it ring again.

Sydney forced herself to walk slowly toward it—across

the the small room, past Lars whose face contorted at her passing.

On the third ring she took the phone, holding it unsteadily with both hands.

At the warmth of Ted's voice came a sudden rush of tears.

"Did I waken you?" he asked, a fine stream of electronic sounds weaving behind his brisk question.

"No," she faltered. "No."

Don Sexton was there, his eyes hostile on hers. She stared at him and spoke breathlessly. "Ted, Don Sexton is here . . . He'll tell you."

"My attorney," she explained, handing the phone to the policeman. Then she turned and fled, the waves of nausea green behind her throat.

By the time she returned, the phone was on its hook. Lars, puffed and strained, was staring numbly into the blankness of the kitchen wall.

"I've called for a team," Sexton said quietly. "Your attorney will be on the next plane. You and I need to talk."

Lars stirred from his lethargy and started, as if to rise, then slumped again. His eyes had almost disappeared in the dull swelling of his face. Brief anger flushed in his eyes, then flickered and died at Don Sexton's warning glance.

"Are you better now?" Sexton asked.

Sydney nodded. "I'm sorry," she said. "I couldn't—"

"Understandable," he said flatly, with no hint that he understood. "I need to know what happened here tonight."

As she looked at him, the long tunnel of past time seemed to join invisibly with the future. With startling clarity she saw the crisp dust-laden leaves of the trees that lined the road from this house to his office in the police station, saw the room with its stiff chair and the white old man with the flexible fingers, heard their questions and the way her answers slid away from their belief like minnows from a probing hand. "I didn't kill Lena Jensen," she said dully. "I didn't kill John Fast. I didn't kill Wagner."

Suddenly she was shaking and could not will her body to stop. After that the tears came, with slow jarring sobs that began somewhere deep inside her, forcing her body into spasms of pain.

Don Sexton stared at her speculatively.

"We'll wait until your attorney comes," he decided aloud. He paused, "But you'll have to come down with us now, you know."

"I'll dress," she said, starting upstairs.

From behind her in the kitchen she could hear the low grumble of Lars' voice, dull with grief. "First that man. Then the dog. Now Lena." His voice rose at the end in a spasm of disbelief. Sydney paused on the stairs, weighed down by a sense of defeat. At Sexton's glance she breathed deeply and began to mount again.

She had forced herself to concentrate on Ted Cross. He was coming, lean and brown from the Arizona sun. Ted Cross would come from John's lost years and help her.

It was then that she remembered. She went to John's desk and opened the drawer to get out the envelope marked "Personal." It was not there on top where she had left it. But Lena had cleaned. She had rearranged things, that was all. Frantically Sydney went through the drawer, once and then again. Then she emptied the two other drawers in the desk and pulled everything from the pigeonholes.

A sense of panic filled her. Her memory had deceived her. She had only *meant* to put the envelope in John's desk.

She groped among the sweaters at the end of the closet and brought down the metal box. There on the unmade bed she opened it.

There were those other things—the title to the house and the house insurance and the car title—but the envelope was gone. The long smooth manila envelope carefully sealed and marked "Personal" in John's clear hand was gone. She pulled her vanity chair to the closet and searched among the sweaters, maybe she had just tossed it back up there, not put it in the file again at all.

In an agony of terror she searched the drawers of the dressing tables—her own and John's. This room—it had to be in this room. She sat on the bed, pressing her palms hard against her flaming temples ordering herself to remember. Remember!

It was no use. She could remember standing there with that brown envelope in her hand and how the memories of her own invasion of privacy had come back to her. She had remembered herself at thirteen with her mother's eager searching eyes on her. She had been unable to invade John's privacy even in death. But how had she hidden it so thoroughly that she could not even find it herself?

She buried her head in her hands and lay across the bed.

After a long while Don Sexton came for her and led her away.

14

So little had changed. Sydney was given the same chair as before. A twin angle of light slid across the desk and spilled into a rectangular pool on the floor where her eye naturally fell. The small vase on the desk that had held a branch of pyracantha berries was now filled with a spray of leaves from a liquidambar tree. A feathery tracery of veins was clear and sharp in the scarlet leaves.

Ted Cross was there. But that change somehow seemed small too. Ted's presence in the room was so weakly felt that Sydney felt the old torpor settling on her again like a poisonous dust sifting through the air. Strangely, Lena's death didn't matter. Sydney tried desperately to make it matter to herself, reminding herself of the children, of the fury of Lars' devotion. But the only reality in the room was the sheaf of reports in Don Sexton's hand binding her to a guilt they had decided was hers.

"Your contacts with Mrs. Jensen during your absence," Don Sexton pressed.

"I called her from San Francisco."

"She knew you were leaving?"

Sydney shook her head. "Only by the note I left."

"And what did you say in the note?"

That note was impossible to reconstruct. Who keeps a carbon of a note to a housekeeper. "I told her I was going to the city to see an attorney," she said. "And that if you called to tell you where I was. And about Wagner."

"Wagner?"

"My dog."

"What about the dog?"

"That he was gone."

"Not killed, not dead—just gone."

"It was easier that way."

"Nothing else in the note?"

"Maybe that I would keep in touch."

"And you called from San Francisco?"

Sydney nodded.

"Please reply verbally for the record," he instructed.

"I called from San Francisco," she said docilely.

"And when was that?"

"Probably about twelve-thirty on Wednesday," she said.

"And you called her house?"

"I called my own home first, thinking she would be working. When there was no answer, I called the valley house."

"Mrs. Jensen was there?"

"No," Sydney corrected him. "I talked to someone else—a friend of hers who said she would give Lena my message."

"What was the message?"

"That I was going to Phoenix and would see her Friday morning."

"Not what flight you would be on?"

She paused, remembering. "She said something about

Lena meeting me, but I explained it was a late Thursday night flight and I had my car."

"Then Mrs. Jensen knew that you were actually coming home last night?"

"If her friend told her," Sydney explained. "I don't know whether she told her that or not."

He looked at her steadily a moment before his questions began again.

"You had no other contact with her or her family about your arrival?"

She hesitated that barest minute. "Not about my arrival," she said. "I did try to call again, from Phoenix."

"When was that call made?"

"On Thursday morning I called her at my home again, but she wasn't there."

When he waited she went on. "So I called the house again and talked to Lars."

"Was this about your arrival schedule?"

"No," she said slowly. "It was something else."

"Would you like to tell us what that conversation concerned?"

Ted broke in for the first time. "Only if you wish to, Mrs. Fast," he said softly.

She stared at him, her eyes thoughtful. "It doesn't matter. It was just an idea that I had. I wanted to know if Lena had used my car that night . . . that night before John. . . . I asked Lars to have Lena think about it."

"Did she often use your car?"

"Not often," Sydney corrected, "but occasionally. Her own car stopped without warning. John had an extra key made for her because it was more convenient for us that way."

"She carried this key all the time?"

"I have no way of knowing," Sydney said. "It didn't matter. We seldom used the car at night."

"This extra key—this extra availability to the murder car—why was this never mentioned before her death?"

"I didn't think of it. It never even crossed my mind until I was trying to think the whole thing through that morning in Phoenix."

"Did you then think that perhaps it was Mrs. Jensen driving the car the morning of your husband's murder?"

Sydney was aghast. She stared at him a moment in bewilderment. "Good Lord, no! I only thought that if she had made a mistake . . . left the key in the car so that anyone coming by . . ."

He changed the course of questions.

"Describe your actions last night."

"I took a plane in Phoenix about four-thirty." She glanced at Ted and he nodded. "It stopped in L.A. In San Francisco I transferred to Air West for Monterey."

"Wouldn't it have been simpler to have flown directly from L.A. to Monterey, since you had to change planes anyway?"

She flushed. That was so obvious. "It would have been, but I had set it up the other way. I simply took the first schedule they suggested."

"So you flew from Phoenix to L.A. to San Francisco to Monterey, arriving at what hour?"

"About ten-fifteen, more or less."

"Baggage wait?"

She nodded. "Only a few minutes," she said.

"So you immediately went to your car and started home?"

She nodded.

"Thirty minutes more or less?"

"I guess so," she said lamely. "I didn't check. When I next noticed the time I was almost asleep. The clock downstairs struck the hour—eleven, I guessed."

Over and over he asked her to describe her examination of the house, what rooms she had entered, was anything changed?

"The security lights weren't on," she said suddenly. "I noticed it when I first drove in. Lena always turned those lights on when she left. But the house was dark."

"Had she ever failed to turn them on before?"

Sydney felt a flash of irritation.

"How would I know? It's one of those household things. Whoever thinks of them turns them on. I know I have; I suppose John has. But usually Lena did."

Sydney's mind began to retreat from the drone of his voice. There were questions about the wine cellar—how frequently she entered it, who had knowledge of its presence there behind the pantry door.

"But there was nothing strange about the house except the absence of lights when you entered it?"

Suddenly she remembered. She looked at Ted. "I think a personal file was gone from my room upstairs."

Since she was looking at Ted, she did not for a moment register the silence that followed her words. When she glanced at Don Sexton he had that expression again, the same expression he had when she'd told him of finding Wagner dead, when she told him about Lena having her own car key.

"So *now*"—the emphasis was unmistakable—"you are telling us that something was stolen from the house in your absence? Is that so? Do you believe that the house was broken into?"

"I don't *believe* anything!" she cried. "The file was

there when I left. Last night it was gone."

Don Sexton sighed. Without moving he seemed to withdraw from Sydney, to dismiss her from his attention. His hand moved automatically to the sheaf of papers on the desk. Almost without glancing at them, he touched them delicately as he spoke. His voice was coming from that great emotional distance. Sydney felt abandoned, walled off from his understanding.

"Let us reconstruct the events of that day." Don Sexton read slowly, without expression, so that the recital seemed less like a narrative than a cumulative score card kept against Sydney's possible innocence.

"Lena Jensen rose and got her children off to school as usual. She stayed at home late to prepare breakfast for Mr. Jensen, who had just returned from his night's work. Then she prepared to go to the Fast house to work, announcing her plan to stop at a grocery store on the way to obtain more cleaning supplies.

"She left her own home for the Fast house a little after ten A.M. At Higgins' store she parked her car in the lot. After completing her shopping and charging the purchases to the account of Mrs. John Fast, Mrs. Jensen attempted to start her car without success. James Ross, an employee of the store, also attempted to start the car, but he too was unsuccessful.

"Mrs. Jensen called home and asked her husband to drive her to her work. At twelve noon he dropped her at the Fast house and asked what time she wanted to be picked up.

" 'I don't have any idea,' she told him. 'I'm running late because of the car. I got a lot of stuff started that I have to finish up.'

"Mr. Jensen suggested that she call their home when

104

she was ready. Whoever was there with the children could receive the call and make arrangements."

"One moment, if you please," Ted Cross interrupted. "Does that mean that someone was at Mrs. Jensen's home to provide transportation for her?"

Don Sexton frowned and shuffled among his notes. After reading a moment he glanced up. "There was some complexity to the baby-sitting arrangements. A teenage girl was to give the children dinner. A friend of Mrs. Jensen's was to relieve the girl when she returned from her day's activities. Mr. Jensen left instructions for the baby sitter to call him at his work if Lena Jensen needed a ride before her friend, who had transportation, returned to take over the children."

"Thank you," Ted Cross said quietly, returning to his own notes.

"After dropping Lena Jensen at the Fast house, Lars Jensen returned home, read the paper, and played with the children on their return from school. The young baby sitter came in about five-fifteen. Mr. Jensen left the house for his work at five-thirty.

"At nine P.M. Mrs. Jensen called her home to see how the children were getting along. The teenage baby sitter told her they were in bed. When Mrs. Jensen expressed surprise that her friend had not returned, the girl assured her that it was all right. The girl was doing her homework and would be fine until Mrs. Jensen's return. At that time Mrs. Jensen told the girl that she thought she would be through in 'an hour or so' and would call again.

"Shortly after Mrs. Jensen's call (the girl did not note the time), Mrs. Jensen's friend, Mrs. Pilar Loomis, returned. She dismissed the girl and waited there with the children for Mrs. Jensen's call. When she still had received no call at ten-thirty, she called the Fast home. When she received no answer, she became concerned and called Lars at work.

"Lars obtained a man to relieve him and immediately returned home. He called all Mrs. Jensen's known friends in the area, becoming increasingly upset. At almost twelve o'clock Lars drove to the Fast house alone. On seeing Mrs. Fast's car in the carport he went for the police."

Don Sexton raised his eye. "This schedule of events is corroborated by statements from all principals involved.

"The pathologist's report shows that Mrs. Lena Jensen died between ten and twelve. The cause of death was strangling; the instrument was a silk scarf established as the property of Sydney Jenkins Fast, employer of the deceased.

"Sydney Jenkins Fast will appear before the grand jury of the county of Monterey, the state of California, on charge of the first degree murder of Lena Jensen."

Ted had words to say. Sydney had none. A slow droning seemed to fill her head. It was the droning that had begun so many mornings before on the deck above the sea at Big Sur, over the crash of surf and the pip of the gulls. It was the sound of the helicopter beginning its long patient search for the end of her life.

Sydney, separated wholly from any sense of self, sat mutely through the Grand Jury proceedings. The faces of the men were flat, not real faces at all. Even Ted seemed to dwindle to a one-dimensional person whose words hung meaningless in the still air.

106

Only Lars was real. Lars was fury tightly buttoned into an unaccustomed suit.

"Lena knew something. Lena must have knew something. Something about that car and the Hastings man's murder. That's why she killed her. Like the man. Like the dog. She was there every day, Lena was. Lena knew what was going on."

Another place, another time, Sydney might have admired the neat mitering of that box. All four sides were there. Sydney Jenkins Fast had the opportunity; she was the only person in the house with the deceased (who did not expect her arrival). The murder weapon was a silk scarf established to have been a part of Mrs. Fast's wardrobe. Sydney Jenkins Fast had motive. The police had found only three sets of fingerprints in the kitchen and wine cellar: the prints of Lena Jensen, Sydney Jenkins Fast, and on some of the untouched bottles, still heavy with dust, incomplete prints of Graham Hastings, now deceased.

The grand jury brought in a true bill, indicting Sydney Jenkins Fast for the murder of Lena Jensen. Bond was set at one hundred thousand dollars.

"It's not the end of the world," Ted tried to tell her.

"Only my world," she said heavily.

"The bail is no problem," he told her. "The judge put no limits on your movements."

"You mean I should run away?" she asked, amazed.

He caught her chin in his hand and tilted her head up almost forcibly.

"Atlanta, Chicago," he reminded her. "The devil wears regular pants, remember?"

"Ted," she asked wonderingly, "do you know that I

am losing John Fast? Do you know how hard it is even to believe in the people we were?"

"That's because you aren't who you were," he told her flatly. "That Sydney was somebody young and warm and protected . . . and cowardly. Now you're the widow of John Fast, the woman who will bring the devil to his knees. Remember that."

When they left the building, Sydney did not even bother to shade her face from the explosion of flash bulbs. Some time between the long night of talk in Ted Cross's apartment in Phoenix and the handing down of the true bill, she had bought John Fast's obsession.

In youth and ignorance and avarice, young John Fast had made an evil compact. The time of reckoning had come. There was a classical choice of how this story could end. A dullness in Sydney's chest told her which way it would be.

15

Those same measured minutes and hours that had slowed to a dullard's pace during the time of Sydney's shock accelerated with pressure. Time, which had been a neutral fluid through which she had moved lethargically, now surged against her, pressing with a dull pain in the back of her head. She was sickly conscious of the passing of those hours in which Ted Cross made their travel arrangements. She found herself restless in flight, irritated by the smallest things—the relaxed voices of other travellers, the droning of the plane's engine.

I am becoming a heel-tapper, a fretter against barriers, she realized with amazement as she waited for Ted to finish his tedious negotiations with the car rental agency in Atlanta. Hurry, we must hurry, her mind beat at her while she twisted her gloves between hands that somehow were never warm now, but always tingled with the stiffness of cold.

She had seen the folded card in Ted Cross's wallet that enumerated, in a few meager lines, the whole intent of this frantic journey. There was the address of the family in Atlanta, followed by a name that sounded curiously boyish: Jim Ray Allen, and his street address in Chicago.

The third line held only the name of an orphanage in a town Sydney had never heard of in a state she had never seen.

She studied Ted Cross's face covertly, astonished as she had been these past days by the almost treasured familiarity of its lines. Did he believe in what they were doing—really believe? Or was this a pilgrimage, a distraction he had invented to help her endure the diminishing hours that lay between herself and the trial?

After she buckled herself into the unfamiliar car, she forced herself to stare through the window hard, compelling her mind to follow her eyes, to make words of the view, to leave bad enough alone for these few minutes.

Late afternoon had come to Atlanta with a sweet slow rain that polished the incredible green of the lawns along Lenox Boulevard. Camellia buds, already formed for late winter blooming, looked ready to explode at the touch of sun. About the giant pines, green halos of ajuga circled the deep red of needle beds. Forcing herself to project an appearance of serenity, she watched the city flow by the car window.

Downtown the city had changed—giant gleaming buildings had sprouted in among the familiar landmarks —but out here, in the neighborhoods, Atlanta was the same richly verdant world of flowers that she remembered from when she had been in Atlanta with John.

"John and I came here," she thought to tell Ted, silent beside her as he maneuvered the rental car in traffic.

"That so?" he asked curiously. "Business or pleasure?"

"It had to be pleasure—we were never apart."

She flushed at Ted's chuckle. "I didn't mean that the way it came out," she revised lamely. "I mean he had no

110

appointments or anything."

"I understood," Ted laughed. "It's just that . . . with the Hastings family here and all . . ." His voice trailed off.

"What do you really expect to gain from them?" Sydney asked curiously.

"Anything at all would be a bonus," Ted replied. "We know that Graham Hastings was born, what his parents' names were, and that is all really. A great hollow empty place lies in there before that murder in Chicago."

"But wouldn't that be the same with you?" she asked defensively. "If the police were to make a file on you like they did on John, would it say what you did when you were ten or twelve or even fifteen?"

Ted glanced at her. "Not totally, of course, but something. They'd have the school I went to, where my parents lived probably. There is none of that for Graham."

He lapsed into silence.

"John and I came in April," she said absently. "There were azaleas everywhere. The dogwood blossoms floated in the air as if they were unrelated to the dark trees that bore them."

Where had they gone? It seemed like a zoo or a giant park in her memory, but she really didn't remember anything but a giant cyclorama of the Civil War action in Atlanta. A buxom woman with crisp curls and a pointer had made the presentation. Her words still echoed in Sydney's ears: "Again and again and again the hordes of the Union army bore down on the valiant warriors of the Confederacy. Again and again they were driven back." Sydney could hear John's voice later that night as he tried to duplicate the multi-syllabic way she had been able to form that "again," as if some wind of that remembered valor had blown the word itself apart to those separate syllables of stress.

"Buckhead." Ted interrupted her musing. "This area is called Buckhead, so we're drawing near."

Something hard and tight formed in Sydney's stomach. "What can I say to them? What will they expect of me?"

"Nothing but what you are—Graham's widow coming to meet with his family. Isn't that natural enough?"

But Don Sexton's voice was there. "Did you know Graham Hastings?" R. O. Alexander's quick turn from his window, his eyes full on her face. "Have they found the murderer?" Lars' voice. "Murderer . . . murderer."

Forgetting that Atlanta had been burned to the ground more than a hundred years ago, Sydney had once expected the city to be a world of Taras left over from another time. This trip she was less naive. When Ted turned into the circle drive of the old house, weaving his way along the red lane that was formed of something chipped and dark reddish, like nut hulls, she didn't expect the giant rambling house that leaned among its porches at the end.

Immense rhododendrons surrounded the porch and the almost oriental angles of azalea bushes flanked the uneven brick walk.

A girl with a face of polished slate opened the door for them. Sydney had an instant of almost uncontrollable terror. Why did she suddenly feel as if she were going home, that beyond the hall door with its carefully polished cherry wood trim would lie her parents' parlor, complete with covered chairs, a breakfront, and the large Bible with its scarlet marking ribbon?

That she and Ted were to meet the Hastingses in concert was at once apparent. The room seemed filled with thin-legged older women displayed on a semicircle of highbacked chairs. Like a seance, Sydney thought, the gathering of the Hastingses to evoke the late lamented Graham. A white sausage of a dog lay by the fire, immobile as a porcelain copy.

From behind the planted elders a younger man stepped forward, almost eagerly, as if to separate himself from their vintage. He looked about fifty, but the pallor of his complexion and the almost funereal formality of his dress made him seem older.

"I'm Lee Railland." He offered his hand to Ted. "And this must be Graham's little widow."

Sydney nodded helplessly as he took her hand.

His voice was so soft that his words flowed past her understanding. His smile seemed real enough, and she responded to it hesitantly. He closed both her hands in his own protectively. He had somehow been appointed family spokesman. He expressed sorrow for each of them that death had come, as he put it, "in the prime of life." Then, as if this formally expressed sympathy was a ritual act that could be finished and forgotten, his tone brightened.

"My goodness," he drawled half smiling. "We must startle you out of your wits, the lot of us. But that's the way we are, you know, a close-knit family, and we're all here!" His words ended in a soft laugh as he led her toward the row of enigmatic female faces.

"Sydney Hastings, my mother, Amelia Railland. That's Amelia Hastings Railland, of course," he explained. "She was a sister to Graham's daddy, Spencer. That makes her your Aunt Amelia."

To Sydney's astonishment, Amelia Railland pulled Sydney's face to her own in a formalized embrace. "So lovely to meet you, dear," the voice said quietly, but the woman's eyes were level and hostile on hers.

The delicately curled and flamboyantly painted one was Flossie Hastings, whom Lee sickeningly defined as "Uncle Spencer's dear baby sister." Flossie's hand was soft as a child's, and the cheek she pressed against Sydney's face felt moist and spongy, like an inadequately baked piece of bread. Flossie beamed at them both with a coquettish delight, as if they had been designed for her entertainment.

Sydney knew she would never be able to fix the third of the old women in her understanding. Lee mentioned something about Macon, evidently where Maudie Silvers had moved from "to make her home with us." Her connubial linking to the Hastings was so carefully explained that Sydney was lost among the Spencers and the Williamses. She settled at last for the most anonymous of greetings. Maudie Silvers' dark brown eyes were satiny in her tanned face. Her hands looked remarkably old and used, with only a gold wedding band interrupting the fine veined wrinkling. She was a listener. "A poor relation," Ted guessed later. "People on indulgence are relegated to the role of children," he explained, "speaking only when spoken to."

The awkward silence after introductions was relieved by the maid bringing refreshments. The confusing variety of offerings included tea in a handsome silver pot and sherry in a low captain's decanter. A tin of sweet biscuits and a small tray of sandwiches were passed haphazardly; Sydney found herself with a glass of sherry and a green-filled sandwich whose anonymous flavor gave a faintly metallic taste to her sherry.

"Mrs. Hastings"—Ted began determinedly amid the

small fluting comments of Flossie and Maudie's quiet replies—"had a great desire to meet Graham's family." He paused as the man Lee Railland nodded approvingly. "There's so much she didn't know of his youth and even his childhood."

"Perfectly natural, my dear," Flossie rushed in. "How tragic to have lost him so young. Such a dear boy." She paused and glanced swiftly at her sister. "Not that I remember Graham all that well as a boy. Why, I hardly remember my own brother, Graham's father," she giggled. "You know how flighty young girls are."

"We were *all* young," Amelia reminded her tartly. "I was still at boarding school when Spencer went to war."

Sydney clung to the names desperately. Spencer—that was Graham's father.

"He served in France," Lee put in, "in World War One. That is where he met his wife, Nikki."

"Dominique," Amelia corrected him firmly. "Her name was Dominique LeClerque, and they were married before we ever met her."

"She was such a pretty little girl," Flossie put in. "Always laughing. And clothes! My such clothes! She loved parties." A wistful note moved behind her words. Sydney had the sudden weird feeling that Flossie, her wide eyes vacantly staring, had somehow evoked the French girl in the room.

The presence seemed real to Amelia, too, who spoke sharply. "Parties indeed," she concurred. "That was all there was to her—just parties and drives and pretty clothes and drinking. While it lasted."

Lee seemed conscious of his role as interpreter. "After the war my Uncle Spencer brought his French wife home and took a position here for a year or two with his daddy in the bank. It didn't work out too well."

"She gambled," his mother broke in harshly. "No man can keep ahead of gambling debts when his wife flies free as a bird like that one did."

"Now 'Melia," Flossie reprimanded her sister. "She was so young. And such a pretty thing."

"She was a mother and a wife, too, you know," Amelia reminded her. "That poor little Graham, left for the help to raise. The Lord only knows how they made out after the trouble—when they went back over there."

"Over there?" Sydney asked, puzzled.

A conspiratorial exchange of glances passed between the women before Lee broke in. "Uncle Spence and Aunt Nikki took little Graham to France. They lived there through Graham's childhood. Spencer died there in 1929. So tragic to go so young!"

"Then Graham was really raised in France?" Ted asked curiously. "When did they return to America?"

"*She* never came back," Amelia said. "But when the Hitler thing began, Dominique sent Graham home for us to educate."

"That's when I remember the dear boy," Flossie put in. "My, what a handsome young man. So tall. And always smiling like his mother."

"Well he might smile," Amelia said. "Our father was a great believer in family. He left the whole of our family property to that Graham because he was the only one bearing the Hastings name. Daddy kept saying to his dying day that young Graham was just slow growing up because of his French blood." The angle of her eyebrows left no doubt of her opinion of her daddy's judgment on this score.

"He was left-handed, you know," Flossie put in apologetically. "It's always been that way with the left-handed Hastings men. Do you remember Uncle Saul, Maudie? The doctor one in Marietta? What a strange man!"

"They all came to a bad end," Maudie confirmed. "There was the left-handed one from Savannah who went turncoat during the war."

Lee ducked his head either in embarrassment or to hide a smile, Sydney couldn't tell which.

"I'm sure Sydney didn't come to hear us rattle family skeletons," he said gently. "Suffice it to say that my cousin Graham didn't fit in so well, with his different background and all. Grandpa sent him off to private school up by Chicago—a military school."

"He never came back," Amelia said resentfully. "That boy never came back one time. He had some trouble at that school and was enrolled in another one. Then my daddy found out that he'd up and joined the army without a by-your-leave. His grandpa was real incensed that the boy did that, truly incensed for a while." Her tone was almost wistful.

"But his war record was superb," Flossie put in, "and even Papa took great pride in that. To his dying day Papa followed the campaigns up there in his bed, proud to have a Hastings in the front line of Europe in that big war." Her voice trailed off sadly, then she added.

"Papa died up there in that bed. He never lived to see our great victory, when the boys came home and all."

"Graham never did come home," Amelia reminded her sharply. "That's been almost thirty years since he left, and now he's gone. He never came home."

"But we had Lee then," Flossie said with a gentle smile at her nephew. "Lee was the man of the house here for all those years."

"Still is," Amelia put in swiftly. "Just having his own place nearer his work doesn't keep him from being the man of this house, does it, son?"

"Of course not, Mother," Lee said, flushing slightly. Then in explanation, "I stayed here with my family for many years then the pressure of my work—"

"The travel," his mother said crossly. "In my day a banker never had to bat around the country like a drummer."

"This is a travelling time," Lee said with obvious embarrassment. "Graham was somewhat of a traveler himself, wasn't he?"

"He stayed in Europe after the war to study," Ted replied quickly. "He was over there a long time."

"You would think he would contact us," Amelia reminded him. "When Daddy's will was read, I couldn't believe what he had done to us. This house and the smallest kind of trust was left to Flossie and me, and the rest all went to Graham. Not once in all those years did he come to see how we were doing, if we were all right."

"He was French," Flossie said lamely.

"And left-handed," Maudie added, without even glancing at them. Her dark satiny eyes seemed focussed on the window behind Sydney's head. "French and left-handed," she repeated almost to herself, as if the combination was too much for her mind to absorb in a single hearing.

"Tell us about Graham," Lee Railland said, leaning toward Sydney as if in apology. "Where did he meet his lovely bride?"

Sydney paused, something hard rising in her throat. She could only see John Fast, lean and strong and silent, moving to the fore of a classroom, his books careless under his arm and his brows knit in thought.

"He was my teacher," she said. "In graduate school."

"Your teacher!" Flossie cried, leaning forward in delight. "How romantic. And you fell in love. That explains how young you are." Flossie's eyes were moist with sentiment, the circles of rouge heightened on her lean cheeks, and her mouth was half open in delight. "How beautiful," Flossie said. "You must have had just a beautiful life together."

"It *was* beautiful," Sydney said. "He was a beautiful person."

Her words fell hollowly in the room. Amelia's resentment was palpable in the air, and the satin-eyed Maudie stared steadily at the stirring curtain, apparently still brooding on left-handed Frenchmen.

The white dog who lay at Flossie's feet rose and turned and lay down again with an almost imperceptible sigh.

Beyond, in the other room, Sydney could hear the maid moving around the kitchen: muted kitchen sounds, a spoon being laid down, a drawer being opened. The scent of food began to stir into the room, warring with the floral-scented cologne that Flossie wore.

Sydney had a weird feeling that young Graham Hastings had come and gone. He had risen, been turned over in their words, and been laid to rest again. The seance was over.

"We mustn't take advantage of your hospitality," Ted Cross said, rising. "I know how much it has meant to Mrs. Hastings that you would receive her."

"She's family," Amelia said, as if reminding Sydney of something.

"I must be getting along, too, Mother," Lee Railland said. "I have a stack of papers that high to go through tonight."

"Surely you can stay to supper," she said. "You've been away so much, Son. Those trips and all."

"Another night, dear," he said, touching her cheek with his. "I'm going to impose on Mr. Cross for a ride to the busline. This rain is never going to let up!"

"Excuse my forcing myself on you like that," Lee Railland said as he joined them in the car. "I thought there might be more specific things you'd want to ask someone."

Sydney turned in the seat. He was a small woman-dominated man, but he seemed sincere. None of his mother's rancor nor his aunt's flightiness seemed to live in him. Once out of that fringed polished room, he had dwindled to a grayness. He was a clerk, a neat humble clerk with pale eyes.

"It did seem a sketchy story," Ted conceded.

"There's been a lot of bad feeling," Lee conceded. "My mother is well past tact about it, I'm afraid. You see, her brother Spencer wasn't a very level sort. The trouble she mentioned was that he embezzled at the bank. Scandal is hard to bury in a close community like this, but Grandpa covered for him, and then sent Spencer and his family to France. The rest of our family—Mother particularly—never felt it was fair for young Graham to inherit the Hastings estate. She never felt he was of us—of them, I mean."

"She has a fair point," Ted said.

"There was another thing," Lee went on. "I don't have

this story too clear because it was all before my time. But Graham got into trouble in Chicago. Something serious about a murder. Because Grandpa was sickly then, the family conspired to keep it from him. It was settled all right—the boy was cleared—but Mother always felt that young Graham owed them something for that. Who knows what Grandpa would have done if he knew? Who really knows?"

It was silent in the car as Ted pulled in at the corner Lee indicated. "We'd really like you to be our guest for dinner," Sydney said suddenly. "Please join us."

Lee's grimace ended in a smile. "I'm just as sorry as anything to have to say no. I'd like having dinner with you people more than just about anything. But I was being honest with my mother about the paper work."

He turned to Sydney with a soft, almost apologetic smile. "I'm in the trust department of the family bank, you see. You might even say that I work for you, Sydney —among others, of course. Grandpa had set up that trust for young Graham long before my time, but I inherited its management. I'm the one that keeps the money rolling in to your bank account. Through Graham, of course."

After extricating himself from the car, he paused for a moment, his hand still on the door.

"I do appreciate your offer of hospitality," he said again. "I get around the country a little on business, like Mother said. If I'm out your way, maybe we could visit again?"

"Don't hesitate," Sydney said quickly, her heart plunging at the thought.

Sydney and Ted Cross watched Lee Railland cross the street as the light changed, a small nondescript man whose shoulders curved under the weight of his dark raincoat.

"There's not much love lost there for the Graham Hastings that I knew as John Fast," Sydney said quietly. There was something poignant about the sight of Lee Railland disappearing into a crowded bus.

"Do you blame them?" Ted asked. "Or him? Maybe him especially. How would you like to live his life, sending a small fortune that you felt should be your own to a faceless account in California?"

"Faceless?" she asked.

He shrugged. "They haven't seen Graham Hastings since high school days. Remember?"

"We learned one small thing about the real Graham Hastings," she said. "John was so right-handed that he couldn't hold a nail properly while he hammered it."

"French and left-handed," Ted muttered in a soft drawl.

Sydney burst into laughter. As she turned to meet Ted's eyes, the unexpected warmth in his face startled her into sudden and uneasy silence.

16

All the way to Chicago the plane moved through layered clouds. The humming of its engines was buried under strains of soft music and a plaintive, repetitive voice that rose and fell in conversation behind Sydney.

Sitting still had become agonizing for her. Her only peace came in movement, restless movement that deluded her into feeling she was not trapped. But the trap was there. "Indicted for the first degree murder of Lena Jensen." She wriggled in her seat and laid her hand on Ted's sleeve for support.

When he turned to her, she was suddenly embarrassed. Her words spilled out nonsensically. "We're moving laterally," she told him. "We're moving back and forth and going nowhere."

Ted laughed softly and recrossed his legs. "I'm sure that the pilot would be astonished to hear that."

"Not the plane, us," she corrected him. "It's like I'm on a leash, like Wagner, able to run back and forth only until Don Sexton gives me a tug, then I'm back there again. I think the Hastings family depressed me. They hated Graham Hastings, didn't they? All of them, even Lee."

"In fairness, it sounds as if they had just cause. That's not a pretty story, you know. If we didn't already have a candidate for murderer, we might well choose Lee. He stands to gain more from Graham Hastings' death than anyone we've seen in the flesh."

Her glance on him was startled.

"Don't make me spell it out," he said. "But take the possibility Sexton makes the murder rap stick—which he won't. . . . Who stands to inherit the estate?"

"The real Graham Hastings," she said.

"That's what I meant," Ted said. "If we didn't already have a candidate. But after Graham, there is only Lee."

She nodded into silence, cross at her own obtuseness. Lee Railland as murderer? Incongruous. He's no more a criminal type than I am, she scoffed to herself. Then the chill hit her. The remembrance of the guilt that had been tailored so neatly about her by the minds of Don Sexton and his staff. And John himself—Good God, if the story Ted told her was true, then John himself in that moment of youthful weakness (she had to think of it as that, there was no other way her mind could contain it) had been guilty of obstruction of justice. But murder? She shivered and leaned closer to the warmth of Ted Cross's shoulder.

"All right?" he asked gently.

"I'm losing faith, Ted," she admitted. "In the big things, like justice and truth and John Fast. Do you realize that?"

"You don't change things by changing their names, Sydney," Ted reminded her. "You and I knew John Fast. Calling him Graham Hastings doesn't change that."

Oh, but it does, she told herself in stubborn silence.

By drifting into death as Graham Hastings, John Fast had washed the wholeness of his life with her away. Where was the man who had been obsessed with Faust for all those years? John Fast had been a shell, an image that he had projected for a magical seven years. John, on whom she had leaned so heavily, had been as empty as herself; a collection of conditioned responses manufactured from the whole cloth of terror. John was nowhere, not in her heart even, she decided guiltily. She had been transformed from the sheltered wife of a man she didn't know to a woman indicted for murder, a woman who drank sherry and ate green sandwiches while she flamed with fury and impatience—a trapped quarry. There was no moving forward left. Atlanta. Chicago. Those were only the names of corners within the larger prison of her legal guilt. Sydney Fast, like John leaving the house that bright morning, was already dead. The only difference was, she knew it.

"You've been to Chicago before, haven't you?" Ted asked as he studied a city map with perplexity in the O'Hare coffee shop.

"Forever ago," Sydney replied quietly. "Well, not quite forever. Make that 1971."

"That was the year you and Graham were married, wasn't it?"

She nodded.

"Tell me about it," he said.

"Our getting married or Chicago?" she asked evasively.

He grinned at her. "Start with Chicago. This is my first trip."

"It was cold," she remembered aloud. "The wind off

the lake chilled our bones. We both hated the noise of the El so much that we moved from one hotel to another trying to escape it."

Only after Ted had obtained a rental car and they were following Ted's carefully marked route through the city, did Ted bring up the subject of that other trip to Chicago again.

"That first trip here doesn't sound like the happiest kind of a holiday," he suggested.

"It wasn't a holiday really," Sydney said. "It was more a flight. That was when we were running away from what we had done to ourselves."

Ted was listening now, really listening. Sydney forced herself to go on.

"John had been cashiered, and of course I had dropped out of school. We had hung around his apartment a few weeks thinking things would settle down, that we could maybe walk out of the house just once without the window shades twitching all along the block and the scent of scandal clinging to us. John was edgy and resentful . . . 'We need awayness, by ourselves,' was what he said. 'For anonymity, you have to be among lots of people.' He chose Chicago." She shrugged.

"Were you married then?"

She shook her head. "I wouldn't do it. John wanted to right off when the stories first started, before the dean even called him in. He wanted us to marry that instant and take off the heat, but I wouldn't."

"Any particular reason?"

"Rebellion mostly, I think. I must have been a little retarded about things like that. I never like being forced into important things. I wanted our relationship to be what we wanted, not what someone said we must have."

"And John?"

"He was a man used to compacts," she said. Had this Faust obsession been where the word had come from? Whoever heard of a contract with the devil? "I, Beelzebub, party of the first part, do hereby pledge to John Fast, who will be hereinafter referred to as party of the second part. . . ." With the devil one would make a compact. The word made a certain archaic sense to her in that context.

"You always do that," Ted said almost angrily. "We'll be in the middle of a conversation and you go off in your head and shut me out."

"I'm sorry." Sydney pulled herself back. "I was thinking about John's soul—or identity, as he called it. What identity, what essence would he have had if none of this had happened at all?"

"That one gets the unanswerable question award," Ted said quietly. "We're really almost here. Watch for number Ninety-Seven."

Business had turned to industry and industry to highrises, only to crumble slowly block by block into a great vertical wasteland of bleak apartment buildings staring at each other window to window along cluttered streets. It was cold. Two children stopped their street play at the approach of the car. Their faces were pinched and angry above shabby denim jackets and worsted mittens.

Number Ninety-Seven was distinguishable from its neighbors only by uneven numbers fastened to the left of the entryway. The solid brick building was ugly and square with chipped gray trim. A patina of smoke and dirt clouded the closed windows. A fire escape rose uneasily along the side, seeming inadequate to support the weight of the trash barrels and refuse sacks that blocked its landings. As if in testament to its inadequacies, the earth beneath it was littered with broken glass and disfigured cans. The wind caught at a piece of loose paper that struggled indecisively, giving the trash itself a sense of liveliness. Ted pulled into the curb, locking the car carefully against a ring of instant curious faces.

A muted bell sounded deep within the house. The ancient green sign on the door read "Manager" in slightly raised letters that had once been white but now were the same drab ecru as the painted walls of the hallway.

After what seemed a ridiculous wait, Sydney heard a faint shuffling from within, and the clank of a chain as the door edged open a careful inch.

"Whatcha want?" The voice was as sexless as the question. A sharp scent was released into the hall by the open door.

The manager's dinner would be chicken, Sydney decided. She could imagine the great bird simmering in its pot, its skin curling back from the legs as clots of fat glistened on the surface.

"We're looking for a man," Ted called through the hostile opening.

"So?"

"His name is Jim Ray Allan," Ted said. "We were given this address."

The chain clanked grudgingly as the door was opened. Sydney guessed the woman who filled the door's width to be in her sixties. From her marcelled hair to her felt slippers she represented the triumph of gravity over human flesh. Her jaws sagged in curved loops over the round wrinkled neck, and from the arm that held the door open a loose wing of flesh moved gently as if stirred by an unseen wind.

"You come too late," she said. "He ain't here."

Ted hesitated. "Is he at work then?"

Her lips tightened briefly as a sudden moisture appeared in her eyes. She loosened the chain as she shook her head.

"He's dead, God-rest-his-soul," she said. "Strange how you should come asking for him. Like they always say, the flowers don't come till you can't smell them. He lived here all them years and there was never a letter nor a caller coming to ask and then as soon as it's too late." Her voice trailed off sadly.

"Dead?" Sydney asked, not meaning to interrupt but unable to contain her astonishment. "Where? How?"

The woman sighed and shook her head again. "At his work, wouldn't you know? A man goes out to make an honest living and they're waiting there for him. It happens all the time," she assured Sydney almost maternally. "Night watch he was. They make a big thing of how a cop or a fireman is a hero in his work, but you just watch the papers. Why, they pick off night watchmen just like flies. Dangerous work. His luck ran out, I guess."

"We are so sorry to hear that," Ted said. "Had he lived here long?"

"You might as well step in," she decided after a searching glance at the kitchen. "Just let me fasten that chain up behind you."

When she had waved them into chairs, the manager lowered herself into an overstuffed chair whose springs had been broken to accommodate her bulk. Sydney perched uneasily by a piano stool, which held an immense thrusting potted fern.

"We sort of inherited him with this place when we bought it," she explained to Ted. "He was here when we came, and we was glad to have a tenant like him. He was a quiet gentlemanly sort, not given to drink or carousing. Me and my Henry—my late husband—we bought this place with Henry's mustering-out pay. Figured it would make us a living through good times and poor. And it was good to its promise. Not all roses and honey," she admitted. "But we survived, fighting the street gangs and the painters with every man Jack of them out for your teeth. But we been here . . . well, going on thirty-five years. Mr. Allan stayed with us right up to his end. Never caused no trouble, so he stayed. You knew Mr. Allan?"

"No," Ted replied honestly. "But he was close to Mrs. Fast's husband. We were looking him up for old time's sake."

"It's just too bad that you missed him," she said. "And by so little. It was the same with his other friend . . . Poor fellow—he come looking for Mr. Allan and I sent him down to the warehouse. He came back—the friend did—pale and shaken and told me the bad news. That Mr. Allan had been shot by some burglars. I fixed coffee for him and we sat awhile, mostly talking about the ways of life, how one morning you're fine and then," she snapped her heavy fingers with a crack that nearly sent Sydney off her chair. "Henry went like that, too, but mercy to God, not by violence. Choked on his dinner he did: choked and coughed and sputtered, said he was fine and then"—she glanced at a narrow door across the dark hall—"went right into that bedroom and died."

Sydney shook her head in sympathy, unable to find words to fit her need.

"It could have been lots worse," the woman said comfortingly. "He might have been afflicted some way and hung on. You know the contraptions they use—the wires and the tubes and all in the nose. It's a mercy when a body can die at home quick among his loved ones."

Sydney's mind slid away to an evocation of the life of this woman and her late Henry. But her mind refused to transform the woman into a girl, young and appealing. Instead she saw John and herself and her discrete demands on life, the sanctuary of that solitary house against the thunder of the sea. All lives are the same, she thought, sheltering unexpected worms in the heart of the apple. The peaceful house in Atlanta, as sleepy as the dog by the hearth but silently blazing with Amelia's sense of being unjustly used. This woman and her Henry having earned the peace of age, only to have it destroyed by the whimsy of death. John's demon forcing him to the edge of the cliff.

She roused herself forcibly to listen to the drone of the woman's voice answering Ted's questions.

"Do you remember this gentleman's name? The one who came to see Mr. Allan?" Ted was asking.

She frowned. "I know I should have wrote it down, but he said it so quick, and once we got talking it seemed rude to ask again. He was the most help to me though. He went through Mr. Allan's papers up there," she pointed skyward to Mr. Allan's room. "Sorted things out —some for the Salvation Army and some he thought I might like to keep for old time's sake. The papers and stuff like that he had carted away. He was a real friend to Mr. Allan."

"But you haven't seen him since?" Ted asked.

"Oh, land no, he was from away. He was only in town for that day and thought he'd look Mr. Allan up.

Couldn't even stay for the funeral. But he left money to buy flowers for the services."

"But no name?" Ted asked.

"No name." She shook her head. "But he was a nice gentleman—you could tell that. Not a man you'd pick from a crowd, you understand, but soft spoken and very easy to talk to. His card read 'From an old friend.' It was kind of touching. Twenty dollars," she added, still impressed.

"Did you tell us when this was?"

She frowned. "The new renter has been in that room there from September on. There was only a week in there that it was empty. Must have been the last week of August . . . Around that."

Ted looked at Sydney unhappily. "It's just very sad to have to go back with this news to John. I wish we could get more details about Jim Allan's death, just to satisfy his mind."

The woman pursed her lips thoughtfully, then heaved herself from her chair. "There's his friend, Mr. Poindexter. He probably still works down there where Mr. Allan did. They were real chums. Maybe you could talk to him."

"That would be very helpful." Ted smiled at her.

She fished a stub of blue pencil from a drawer in the roll-top desk. "I'm sure it's Poindexter," she repeated. "An old man, like Allan. Just ask there at the warehouse. Somebody's supposed to be there all the time."

An acrid burning scent came from the kitchen as she let them out.

"Her dinner is burning," Ted whispered as he smiled his way down the stairs with the woman still watching from her doorway.

"No," Sydney disagreed. "She put a lid on the chicken and it's boiling out. She'll just have a stove top to clean."

"She got your sympathy," Ted commented as he opened her door.

"She's sort of sad," Sydney said. There wasn't any point in telling Ted how the interview had affected her. A dullness lay heavily in her chest. The woman was a quarry, like herself, waiting for days to pass, waiting for death to come, hoping it was swift like Henry's. Waiting like Sydney herself was waiting for the trial, knowing the end was coming, hoping that it might somehow come gently.

"Off to Poindexter," Ted said, glancing up at her from the map.

The warehouse was not easy to find. After a series of false starts, Ted finally got onto the road that wound back through industrial plants and abandoned buildings to the old rickety building. The day was drawing to an end. The chill wind of early evening whipped fiercely around Sydney's ankles as they fought their way across the littered parking lot.

A small glassed-in office held the dark at bay in one corner of the cavernous lower floor. The small man who rose from his books at their entrance stared at them with interest through giant glasses. Sydney noted that the lines of his face all pointed the right way, crinkling into an instant and infectious smile at Ted's greeting.

"G'dafternoon," he slurred as he nodded to Sydney. "Help you?"

"We're looking for a man named Poindexter."

The man nodded cheerily. "He's here. He's here." He glanced at a row of time cards staggered on nails against his wall. "Be off in three quarters of an hour. Are you in a hurry?"

"Not that much hurry," Ted replied. "Do you have a minute?"

The old man laughed, "Time is all I do have. The numbers will wait, you know. You post and post and next day they come up again. May not mean the same, but they're the same numbers. Sit, miss?"

"We're on the track of an old friend of ours," Ted said. "We just heard this afternoon that he was killed on the job here in late August."

"Jim Allan." The man's face darkened. "Rotten shame. Fine fellow. Good worker. Nice guy." With each succeeding sentence his voice dropped delicately until at the end his tone was almost sepulchral.

"What happened, Mr.? . . ." Ted paused.

The old man leaned over briskly and turned up a small neat plastic sign. "Bellows," he said tersely, "Dan Bellows." Then he leaned back and placed the tips of his fingers together carefully so that his nails barely met. He studied this pattern of joined tips a minute, then shook his head.

"He was a watchman, you know—night watchman." Ted nodded. "He'd come on duty about six. The loaders had already left and he checked in like usual. Used to be we had two men working here nights. But that was when the shipments were finished clothes. We're in men's fine tailored suits, you know," he said proudly. "But they've changed things around. We handle only the bulk goods: linings, cartons, and such. There's not the temptation to robbery like the old days. Allan was on alone like usual, doing his rounds.

"We'll never know what happened. There was a door

broke in, but the inventory didn't show anything missing. Not so much as a package of pins, as they say. But there was Jim Allan lying in his blood there in the back of the second floor."

"Who found him?" Ted asked.

"The cop on the beat," Mr. Bellows said. "He happened to see that busted door and tried to holler him up. When he didn't get an answer, he came in to check."

"And they never found out who did it?"

"Never even got a suspect that I heard," Mr. Bellows said. "Whoever done it could have cleaned this place out by the time the cop came. But there wasn't a thing gone —not a pin." He shook his head confusedly.

"That's a strange and sad story," Ted agreed. "An old friend of his died recently and left him a bequest. Do you know who his heirs were?"

The old man turned and dug in a low green file drawer. "Unless you can find it in his records, I wouldn't know. He was with us forever, you know. When he was young he worked over in the main plant, where they make the suits. He was there from well before the war. He was never called on account of a limp he had. He was retired over there with a pension even. But he was at loose ends without anything to do." The old man grinned. "Not that I don't understand." He pushed his books almost affectionately. "I fuss at them books and curse them, but you wait. The minute I don't have them numbers to work with, I'll be as restless as a lean hen. In any case, they let Allan come back—just night watching, but something to do.

"Here, go through this file if you please. A bequest, eh? Too bad Jim Allan never saw that. It would have made him feel good to know somebody remembered."

Sydney stared out into the empty warehouse as Ted worked his way through the Jim Allan file. The light within their cubicle seemed to brighten as darkness filled the wide cavernous room.

Occasionally Sydney caught a word or a date that Ted absent-mindedly whispered aloud as he made notes from the files. A steady fine screech came from Mr. Bellow's pen as he totted his columns and turned the heavy green pages to begin totting again.

As the whine of a lift sounded in the great room outside, Mr. Bellows raised his head. "That'll be Poindexter now," he told Ted over his shoulder.

Sydney watched the old man approach the office to check out. Behind her Ted was thanking Mr. Bellows for the use of the file and the time he had given them.

She was turning the knob to go out when she heard Mr. Bellows' easy voice speak in a confused, almost angry tone.

"There's something else I wanted to say," Mr. Bellows spoke swiftly, as if to get the words out before Mr. Poindexter entered the room. "It's always bothered me, but there was nothing to do about it. The company sent me out that next morning to tell the folks where Jim Allan lived and all. Poindexter was the obvious man, but he was real broke up . . . real broke up when Allan was shot. So they sent me.

"There was an old woman there where he lived. And she already knew. I never could get anyone to understand how wrong that hit me. Some fellow, a soft-spoken fellow who passed himself off as a friend of Allan's, had been out there going through his things. When I got there his stuff was all in neat piles ready to be taken out so the place could be let again. He'd come the night

136

before, she said, a little before eight.

"What's so fishy is that Jim wasn't even found until the cop made his midnight round here. How come he knew? I ask myself. How come he knew?"

Ted and Mr. Bellows stared at each other as the door opened and Mr. Poindexter came in, nodding at Sydney as he passed.

17

Mr. Bellows managed to give an air of informality to the introduction. "I have been visiting here with these friends of Jim Allan's," he said companionably. "I think they'd like to talk to you."

The man looked at Ted hard before his eyes flicked to Sydney. He was small and soiled from his work. A meagerness about the flesh of his face spelled ill health or fatigue, but there was a fierce energy in the way his eyes searched Ted's face.

"You want to talk to me." It was less a question than a challenge thrown like the opening prod of a contest.

The open hostility in the man's voice as he spoke to Ted startled Sydney. Along with her instinctive withdrawal from his rudeness, her intuition told her that Poindexter was not a man who would confront a woman that harshly. She caught Ted's startled glance as she stepped forward.

"I wanted to talk to you," she said. "I just lost my husband, you see." She forced the words to flow out evenly so he would have no opportunity to demur. "In his will my husband, Graham Hastings, left a bequest to your friend, Mr. Allan. We came here to see Mr. Allan, all this way, my attorney and I, and then we got the awful news."

He was listening carefully, weighing her and the words and the sense behind the words, weighing and not deciding. Sydney felt Ted stir behind her, only the barest movement, but she leaped in again to stall him off.

"You see, Mr. Poindexter, we hadn't been married all that long. I didn't know any of his friends. I decided to come myself. Do you understand?"

He only stared at her steadily, speculatively.

"You said you was married to Graham Hastings," he said finally. "But you didn't say which one."

Sydney felt a sense of shock at his words. She was groping for words when Ted interrupted.

"Look, Mr. Poindexter," Ted said persuasively. "We know you're tired, that you just came off duty. But Mrs. Hastings does need to talk to you—to some friend of Jim Allan's. Could we buy you dinner or a drink, or both?"

The old man stared at Ted and then at Sydney a long moment before shrugging. "I'm not for sale for food nor drink, but talk comes cheap. You been here before, fellow? You ever been here before?" His voice was wary.

"Never," Ted said. "Maybe that's why this damned Chicago wind is taking my hide off."

Mr. Poindexter looked at him and shrugged again. "Talk's cheap," he repeated. "My car's out there."

"Is there a place nearby where we can sit and be out of the wind?" Ted asked.

"My place ain't far," Poindexter said without gusto. "It's there or no place."

Poindexter's place was a walkup on the fourth floor of an apartment building whose exterior was not perceptibly different from the one Jim Allan had lived in. The difference began at the door. Mrs. Poindexter, a bland-faced, round-eyed woman in her seventies, rose with dignity as they entered. "Gracious, Deck," she said uneasily. "You could have told me we had callers. Come in, miss." She nodded to Ted.

"They come to talk about Jim," Mr. Poindexter said, throwing his cap so that it caught and circled and finally hung on a turned wooden knob on the hatstand in the hall.

"Wasn't that just the most dreadful thing?" Her voice thickened with fear. "I fret all the time about Deck out there. The streets of this town."

"It's all towns," Ted told her. "Please don't let us delay your supper. I feel bad about intruding."

"Oh," she waved airily, "Deck's not one of those who rush in to grab a spoon. He needs to sit a spell and gather his wits. But I'll leave you to your talking."

All the warmth left the room at her bustling departure. The men sat across from each other, waiting.

"You confused me a little back there," Ted said finally. "What did you mean by 'which Graham Hastings'?"

"I spoke over-fast when I said that," Mr. Poindexter said almost apologetically. "But I'm still upset about Jim Allan. You might understand that—him and me being best friends for such a long time. And that name, that Graham Hastings name, brought back the old times all of a rush when I wasn't prepared for it."

"I'm interested in the old times," Sydney said. "I'm interested in what you said about two Graham Hastings."

"It's all pure hearsay," the old man said. "There was only one man by the name, even if two men used it."

"How did that come to be?" Sydney asked, leaning towards him.

Mr. Poindexter sighed and then shook his head. "I know and then I don't know. Peg"—he nodded towards the kitchen—"knows as much as I do or more. I was off at war when it came about. The most I know was Jim Allan talking about it all those years. Nothing much ever happened to Jim, you see," he explained. "He was gimpy from polio as a child and was never let go fight. He never married, worked for the same company all his life. Why, he even lived in the same flat for near forty years. That made the Graham Hastings thing a big deal in his life."

His wife's voice from the doorway broke in with a tone of annoyance. "What's all this about Graham Hastings?" she asked her husband pointedly. "The past bury the dead, is what you better do. Leave it be."

"This girl tells me she is Graham Hastings' widow," Poindexter said, looking at his wife very straight. Something wordless passed in their exchanged glance, a fiercely tender challenge that Sydney could not understand.

"I was fixing to tell them about it," he added.

"What good will it do?" Peg asked him, almost angrily.

"She wants to know," he said.

"Why?" she asked Sydney, her jaw squared.

Sydney didn't look at Ted. She didn't dare. She looked down at her hands, startled to see them twisting John's ring rapidly, almost painfully. With studied effort she folded her hands and bid them be still.

"We've lived out on the coast for five years," she began. "Graham and I. Then three weeks ago he was killed by a hit-and-run driver. It wasn't a real accident—

the police know that. I need to know more about his past. I need to know who killed him."

"We can't help you," Peg said quickly, looking at her husband hard, her eyes rounder than ever in her pale face.

"I just need to know," Sydney pleaded. "I need to know what happened back here."

"And about the two Graham Hastingses," Ted reminded them.

Peg Poindexter stood in the doorway, her lips pressed tightly together in angry silence. Mr. Poindexter, after a quick sheepish glance, looked away from her and began.

"Jim Allan and me was high school friends back in Joliet. We never lost touch even after he come to Chicago and went with the company. After Peg and I was married, I took a job here, and we saw Jim now and then. He and I'd have a beer, or he'd come over to jaw with Peg and me. He was always a lonely sort, back in high school and after he was a man. But he seemed to like coming here.

"He did have one friend down at his work, a boy he called Will. A lot of times he brought the boy along to our place.

"A big, rangy, quiet kid. Jim Allan thought a world of that boy and we liked him, too." He glanced towards his wife for affirmation only to look back swiftly.

"When Will quit coming along with Jim, Jim told us the kid had got himself a real buddy. Jim laughed because he said them boys was like two peas in looks. You had to know them real well to tell Will from this Graham Hastings. Jim didn't cotton to Graham Hastings, but Peg and me figured he was just jealous, him and Will having been such friends and all.

142

"The war was heatening up then, and I got my papers even though Peg was expecting. When I left, Peg was to stay on here until her time and then go home to her folks in Joliet to bear the child.

"Jim was real good to Peg those months after I left, and that's when it all happened. I've heard Jim Allan talk about it often enough, but Peg was here." He looked at his wife almost pleadingly.

She stared back at him sternly, her mouth tight with annoyance.

"You wouldn't be telling anything that hasn't been told a million times," he reminded her petulantly.

Instead of answering, she retreated to the kitchen with her back set full to her husband. He watched her go and then shook his head. "You'd think I'd understand that woman by now, wouldn't you?" he asked. Then he sighed and stared down at his hands.

"Well, Jim Allan was good to Peg. Carried in her heavies and checked the place over and sometimes got her to the doctor and back, travel being hard those times. Jim talked to Peg a lot about his friend, Will, and this Graham Hastings. Graham had took up with some girl that Jim thought was pure poison. Her name was Clara, or something like that. Later when Jim described her to me he said she looked almost Indian—short and light-boned with a lot of heavy black hair and her eyes shaped funny and too far apart. But she must have been a looker, because Jim said so, and he wasn't the sort of man who generally noticed.

"Well, just about the time Peg went off to Joliet because the baby was come due, that girl was murdered. Peg sent me pictures from the paper. It was a nasty one all right." He glanced at the kitchen and lowered his voice. "She'd been living with another girl, and from what they said it wasn't like two girls should have been together. They call them lesbians now and say it right out, but in them days it was something way out of the ordinary. And all this time she was running with this Graham Hastings and him paying her bills and meals and all.

"According to the papers I saw, this Graham Hastings come in on the two of them and being a hothead went into a real fit. He knocked the Indian girl out—the one he was living with—and murdered her girl friend. Just flat out strangled her and threw her naked body out in the hall like so much rubbish. Then he walked away like nothing happened."

Mr. Poindexter stirred fretfully. "I wish Peg weren't so spooked out about all this," he complained. "She was right there in the middle and with me it's secondhand.

"But even with the war and all, they gave that murder a lot of coverage. It was what they called cut-and-dried. While nobody had seen Graham Hastings coming in or out that night, the neighbors all knew him and knew what was going on with him and that girl. I don't guess they even looked for another suspect. There were finger-prints all over the place—on the door and furniture—and even some blood stains on the Indian girl he knocked out. So they put a dragnet out for this Hastings, just tearing up the town looking for him.

"That's when the strange thing happened. Jim's friend, Will, disappeared."

"Disappeared?" Sydney asked, perplexed.

Mr. Poindexter nodded. "That's how Jim felt about it. One day he was there, and the next he was gone. He didn't show for work, and when they checked he'd

144

moved out of his rooming place. He just all the way disappeared overnight. Jim figured he was helping his buddy Hastings hide out, but he was still surprised. Will was always a hard worker and dependable, and to go off like that without a word wasn't like him."

"Where did he go?" Ted Cross asked when the old man paused.

Mr. Poindexter grimaced. "I'll let you decide on that for yourself. Jim Allan troubled it for as long as he had breath, but his was only one opinion."

"Did the police ever find Graham Hastings?" Sydney asked.

"Didn't have to," Poindexter said almost triumphantly. "After three or five days—something like that—this Graham Hastings turns himself in as open as can be. Says there was some big mistake, and he was never near the place that night and that was all there was to it.

"The city had a case that it looked like a lamprey couldn't get out of, but it was all based on them fingerprints. When Graham Hastings came in, they took his fingerprints and there wasn't any case left."

"Surely they had copies of his fingerprints before?" Sydney protested.

"Not that young," Mr. Poindexter said. "Graham and Will was both due to report for draft boards, but not processed yet. Like I said, they were kids. And back then they didn't slap your thumb on an ink stamp every ten minutes like they do now, for driving licenses and all."

"And what did Jim decide about all this?" Ted asked.

"Well, you got to remember there wasn't much in Jim's life, and he had lots of time to think. And he read a lot." Mr. Poindexter paused as if embarrassed to go on.

He glanced at Ted shamefacedly. "I ain't saying I buy

145

this, but it was Jim's theory and he was a pretty sharp fellow. He kept turning that case over and over in his mind, putting in a piece here and a piece there until he could make it a story he could live with.

"You see, Will was an orphan and never even ate proper until he was working here with Jim. He used to talk pretty wild about money. Jim remembers his saying that he'd sell his soul for enough money to live like a man instead of an animal. Jim laughed at him. You know how big a kid like that can talk!

"But Jim thought maybe, just maybe, he did that. What if Graham Hastings gave him money, a lot of it, for Will to turn himself in for that murder when the police were digging the town for him? What if he played out the whole string? The neighbors would fall for it. It was usually night when they saw Hastings and, like Jim said, they looked more alike than most twins. If neither of those boys was old enough to be registered in the draft yet, who's to tell whose fingerprints were whose?

"Jim always said that there were two Graham Hastings —the one who got away with murder and the one who was suspected and exonerated of it. It grieved him to think that Will had got himself into a box like that. He used to shake his head and say that a thing like that was never really over—never over as long as a man lived."

Sydney felt her breath leave her body in a long slow painful exhalation.

"Now tell me that ain't a strange story?" Mr. Poindexter challenged Ted almost bitterly.

"That's a strange story," Ted agreed, staring morosely at the floor.

"Since you've gone this far, you might as well tell them about the girl," Mrs. Poindexter said from the doorway.

"It's probably not important," Mr. Poindexter replied, "but it got Jim all upset. Late last summer Jim came by to take supper with Peg and me on his day off. He swore to God that he had seen that girl of Graham Hastings'— Clara or something her name was. He said she was older but still the spit of herself. She was walking down the road there past the warehouse where you got me today. Jim thought to call out to her, but she made such a point of not recognizing him that he didn't do it. Jim was a shy one, anyway. But he watched her. He watched her go down that road to where the dead end is and turn around and walk back. Then a half block or so from the warehouse she got into a car and drove off."

"And when was this?" Ted asked.

"Oh, summer—late August maybe," Peg said. "Not more than a week before Jim was killed."

"And when was Jim Allan murdered?" Ted Cross asked, leaning forward.

"The last of August," Mrs. Poindexter said. Sydney realized that the old woman's hand was white, gripping the back of her husband's chair.

"I told you no good could come of dragging that story up again!" she said.

Ted led Sydney out of the Poindexter apartment in a thoughtful silence that she was first to break.

"Then Jim Allan's murder was linked with John's," she said. "But why?"

"Because Jim Allan was the only man who knew there were ever two Graham Hastings'," Ted said.

"Except Poindexter," Sydney said. "Which makes his wife's fear look pretty sane."

The clock in Sydney's head ticked steadily, numbing the back of her brain. She tried to see young Will in the

John Fast she remembered. He wasn't there. He was nowhere. And the clock was running out.

Graham Hastings had strangled a girl and thrown her out in the hall like rubbish. Graham Hastings had forced John Fast over the cliff into the sea. Surely, surely it was Graham Hastings who had twisted the life out of Lena with an apricot scarf. But Graham Hastings was nowhere —only a name, a faceless name that had set the clock in her head.

For the first time since they'd left California, Sydney gave way to tears.

18

Ted, who had been diligent in rushing her from place to place, seemed to have lost steam. He was busy enough —off on errands, making endless long distance calls in all directions—but seemingly content for them to stay in Chicago for day after dreary day.

Sydney, numbed by recurrent dreams of shadowless light and repelled by the noise and confusion of the city, meekly submitted to long hours in her hotel room alone. He brought her books that failed to engage her mind. He filled the room with fresh flowers that only made her ache for the smells of her own garden.

They were at breakfast in her room. Ted was frowning with concentration at his growing stack of papers, lifting his coffee cup to his lips mindlessly only to stare again and shuffle.

Off in Big Sur, the sea would be curling morning against her cliff while gulls swayed low over the redwood deck. A crust of salt would have formed there, making the deck floor crisp under her feet as she stood barefoot watching the breakers moving in from Japan.

Then Ted lifted his eyes to her. His voice was brisk

with morning. "We are ready to go home," he announced.

The brightness in his voice only depressed her.

"First I will show you the little treasures I have accumulated; then you must tell me that you approve of my plan."

Sydney smiled for him, but inside her own head she spoke to him. "I'm sorry, Ted," she thought. "I'm sorry I ever came to you. We've failed and you don't seem to realize it. You should go back to the blazing sun of Phoenix and your apartment with its wall-to-wall books." Instead she asked carefully. "What is your plan?"

"You might not approve of it."

The warning in his voice intrigued her. "You have bought us 'his and hers' matching tickets to the Orient, and we're going to run away," she suggested.

He grinned and scoffed. "Nothing that easy. Out there we would only have the communication gap and the possibility of cholera. I think big."

Because his eyes on hers were serious and doubtful, she waited.

"That lead in Michigan didn't turn out to be the red herring I had feared." He slid a memo sheet across the table to her. "The orphanage is a small place, run by nuns. According to their records, only three new children were admitted that year. A girl came to them late in winter following a family tragedy, a boy was brought in April, and in the fall the third child, a boy, was found."

"Found?" Sydney asked.

Ted nodded. "The sister waxed quite lyrical about the event. There was a bitter storm and the child not more than a few days' old at most. An old man in his seventies was among a bare scattering of people who came to early mass that morning. A few hours more, and the child might have died from exposure.

"They gave him the birthday of October 23 for his baptismal papers. They named him William Lowery, after the old man who had brought him from the parish church to the orphanage through wind and snow."

Suddenly she could hear John's voice, warm with pleasure . . . see the glint of candles across a mass of low roses. "Fortunate he who is born in the season of the crab. October."

"William Lowery?" she asked, testing the name on her tongue.

Ted didn't look up from his notes. "Excellent school records, good health except for a minor tendency for sore throats . . . broke his leg in a bike accident at nine, tonsils out at eleven and a half. The sister remembered him as an uncommunicative child who was both physically active and good at reading, a rare combination. A change occurred in the administration at the orphanage the year he was thirteen. After that he grew restless. At fourteen and a half, he ran away. They gave no further records on him. He was tall and thin when he left— almost six feet—dark brown hair. 'A good-looking boy,' she said.

"The sister added that his running away was not extraordinary. From fourteen on the boys are hard to hold . . . a restlessness . . ." Ted's voice trailed off.

Sydney thought of that first day John had shown her the lot on Big Sur. It hadn't looked like a lot to her at all, that jagged rocky cliff hanging above the sea as if by sufferance.

"It's beautiful," she had told him, "but so alone."

"Don't you like it?" he had asked with instant concern.

151

"Of course I like it," she had reassured him. "I guess I just expected neighbors—or people close."

"I had all of that I needed as a kid," he had said. "People penned together get calluses on their souls."

Was that what had happened to Will Lowery? Had he grown such calluses on his soul that he would trade it for another man's blood guilt just for the money to escape?

She tried to imagine John as young Will Lowery—the heavy brown hair, the tall slender frame in orphanage clothes. Her mind veered from that.

"That was the first of my small triumphs," he said, as he pulled out another file. "Now see this."

Like most photostatic copies of old newspaper pictures, the prints Ted pushed across to her were overexposed and fuzzy. Sydney studied the girl Clara. Even the poor print managed to catch a sultry attractiveness in the rebellious face. Sydney had the strange sensation of recognising the wide-set eyes that stared back at her. She shivered. She had met women like Clara more than once. She laid the picture aside and studied the lean young man identified as Graham Hastings. "Exonerated," the headline began. It was John Fast. Even with his arm thrown over his face to conceal his features from the camera, she recognised the shape of his lean body, his rangy proportions.

"Graham Hastings né William Lowery," she said. "Jim Ray Allan was right. What plan have you developed from all this?"

Ted's apprehension of her reaction was betrayed by his preoccupation with the papers before him.

"I made a statement for the papers in San Francisco."

His voice was defensive. "I called a reporter that Alexander knows. I gave him a sort of evasive release—just the suggestion that a search was in progress for a man named William Lowery who might have information on the murder of Graham Hastings."

She stared at him. "That's insane. A boy disappears from an orphanage some forty years ago and you advertise for him? What can you hope to gain? How can that do anything but make my trial more of a case for public interest—a playday for curiosity seekers and scandal mongers?"

"Sydney, Sydney," Ted's voice was patient. "Don't take off like that. I've watched you slide away from things all this time. You can't just retreat into anger; you have to look at this thing straight on. Add the numbers and see where we are."

"Numbers," she scoffed. "We have raced from here to there talking to people. We have followed dead trails and found only dead men at their ends, and you talk about numbers."

"Okay, they are not hard numbers, but they do add up. This thing has a shape now, and the missing piece is William Lowery."

She stared at him, angrily defensive.

"Jim Allan's scenario is sound, as you admit. You have two young men who bear a startling resemblance to each other. I have to wonder how they became friends. Could they have come together because of that resemblance? There was little else to bring them together—a runaway impoverished orphan working in a suit factory and a spoiled brat with endless financial resources. They might have first connected through a case a mistaken identity.

That would certainly set the stage for Graham Hastings using this resemblance as a means to escape prosecution for murder."

Ted stopped and studied her a moment before going on.

"And remember how young they both were. Young enough for Graham to lose his mind with rage when he found his girl *in flagrante delicto* with another woman. That strangling was obviously done in a rage of passionate fury—carelessly, with fingerprints everywhere—in a neighborhood where he had been seen in the past and was therefore familiar to any one of a number of witnesses.

"He would have come to his senses and been a very scared young man. There were very few electives. He could run but without much chance of getting very far. It was wartime. It is not easy to be a fugitive young man at a time when every able-bodied male is tagged and numbered.

"He could let himself be caught or turn himself in. That would be a real gambler's try. The least he could hope for, with his record of incorrigibility in schools behind him, would be a long imprisonment. Crimes of passion are sometimes treated gently by courts in the case of a man 'defending his castle.' Illicit relationships were not in that category. Not in those days anyway."

He paused a moment, waiting for her agreement. "Or he could hire a stand-in. If the same witnesses who identified him as Clara's 'young man' would identify the stand-in, and if the fingerprints were the basis of the prosecution's case, both men could go free."

"With a simple switch of identity," she said.

Ted shook his head. "Not that easy. Nobody takes the

chance of turning himself in for a possible murder conviction just out of friendship. Graham Hastings is frantic. He needs a new identity. Graham is willing to trade what he has to offer, the Hastings name and inheritance, for a new identity and life."

"All right. All right." She nodded. "But this has all happened and been over a long time ago. The Graham Hastings who began life as William Lowery and ended it as John Fast is dead. What makes you think that the William Lowery who once was Graham Hastings is going to surface in answer to a newspaper article?"

" 'The man who once was Graham Hastings,' as you put it, knows this name well. If Poindexter is right, he went to Mexico under that guise—William Lowery, American citizen; place of birth, Stroud, Michigan; male; brown eyes and hair . . . the whole bit. But a lot of years have passed. The kind of money that Hastings had is not easy to come by. He begins to regret his bargain.

"Then he tries blackmail, remember? Who but the first Graham Hastings would know to blackmail the man who used his name? And the attempts on his life."

Sydney shook her head. "It's all preposterous."

"Only now," Ted told her, "that's the way with men. The small steps make sense one at a time because of expediency. It's only when all the steps have taken you somewhere like this that you start crying 'preposterous.' One step at a time made sense."

"So it became a battle of wits after that," Sydney thought aloud. "Graham Hastings changed his name, his whole identity, and life-style to elude his pursuer, but without success."

"There's the missing piece," Ted interrupted. "His attempt was successful. Look how long it worked. John went back to school—all the way through his doctorate —and was safe. He married and you had seven years of safety. Now the question rises, how did the real Graham Hastings find John Fast? How did he locate that house on Big Sur, acquire knowledge of your life and John's, and, please God, even get keys to your car? The devil is alive and well along that California coast, Syd, and he knows who we're looking for when we advertise the name William Lowery."

She stared at him a long time. Past her eyes she ran those men's faces that were part of the background of their lives on Big Sur. But there were so few faces—Pablo hacking at the stairs, the tradesmen who were as anonymous to her as the services they offered, Lars, Don Sexton. She shook her head.

"No one," she said. "There's no one at all."

"We'll see," he said firmly, fastening the papers together. "We have to get back home to Big Sur. I need to spend some time with Alexander in San Francisco tomorrow. I want to sift his files, see if there's anything we've missed. There's one link missing still. There's the person or the method by which the devil in whatever name he wears located John Fast on Big Sur."

Sydney moved methodically to prepare for the flight west. Against the drumbeat in her mind, she folded clothes into the white suitcase. She felt a perverse sense of satisfaction when she was through, as if she performed those physical movements by the sheer force of will.

They had been in flight some time. After a broad stretch of prairie, a mountain range pricked upward toward her window, its peaks already whitening with the onset of winter. It was then that she finally trapped the question that had moved stealthily about the corners of her mind.

"Was this all revenge then?" she asked Ted. "How can Graham Hastings possibly profit from John Fast's death? Even from my execution as his murderer—or Lena's?"

Ted sighed and laid his hand on her arm. "Sooner or later you were bound to get around to that. I think the answer lies in a woman named Clara."

"Clara?" she asked almost stupidly.

"Clara," Ted repeated. "Graham Hastings' girl, the one who shared the apartment with her murdered friend. The girl Jim Allan described so persuasively. The girl in the newspaper shots got from the old file—the slender dark girl with the eyes too wide apart and the full mouth."

Sydney stared at him, trying to recall those pictures, but she could only evoke the shot of John Fast as a young man—John, young and defensive against the barrage of photographers, lifting his arm high to shield his face.

"You do remember the message that Ralph Alexander so cryptically mentioned to you?" Ted asked.

She nodded.

"That letter was from a woman named Clara Hastings. She claimed to be the legal heir to her husband's estate."

"My God, that's not possible."

"She enclosed a photostat of a marriage license, issued to herself and Graham Hastings in Mexico City."

She laughed suddenly and bitterly. "That may be the final fem lib twist of the whole wild story—that the devil is a woman after all."

She had more questions. Why Wagner? Why Lena? But Ted's face was gray with fatigue as he stared at the darkening sky, finally letting his head fall back on his head rest.

Sydney stared straight ahead, holding her eyes open hard. Beneath her eyelids lay the dark of her own terror, stirring, moving gently like the waves tugging at Wagner there among the pillared stones.

19

Ted insisted that Sydney spend the night in San Francisco before returning to Big Sur. He tried to persuade her to wait until he finished his business with the attorney, so they could return together.

She replied stubbornly to his unspoken reasoning. "I know it's lonely there, Ted, but it's all the home I have."

She regretted her stubbornness the moment she got home.

She moved through the sunlit rooms numbly. The house had become a collection of alien rooms.

"Don't think about anything," Ted had told her at parting.

Minds aren't like that, she argued mutely as she moved through her house. Minds are like clocks, they go on. But the clock had stopped here.

She tried to remember how John had reset the clock after an absence. She tugged the chains and pushed its hands into place, but the clock remained mute. Finally, on the back, she found directions. In answer to the thud of the door closing, a faint tick came and the hands began their patient circling of the hours.

A patina of dust hazed the dark of her tables. She

moved from room to room, imitating Lena until consciousness of her mimicry drove her outside.

A few blossoms had opened among the iceplants on the hill. It had rained during her absence, and the fog had been heavy enough to waken their scarlet blossoms.

The first telephone ring was another sound against the surf. When it rang again she ran inside, trailing mud across the entryway in her haste.

She didn't recognize the voice at first.

"Miz Hastings," the tone was querulous. "Sydney? This is Lee Railland."

"Lee," she cried. "What in the world?"

He chuckled, "I just knew you'd be surprised. In fact I'm a little surprised myself."

"Where are you?" she asked quickly. "Atlanta?"

He was still chuckling. "As a matter of fact, I'm practically around the corner. You people had just left when this trip came up. I tried to let you know I was coming, but you weren't there yet, so I came on."

"On where?" she asked, still confused.

"Well, I was in Los Angeles this morning, and later I go on to San Francisco, but I stopped off here in Monterey."

"Well, you *are* just around the corner." Sydney felt a quick grip of terror. What if he picked up a paper and read about the trial? My God, must he come now, with the trial only a few days away?

But the carefully conditioned hostess responded automatically. "I will get to see you, won't I?" she asked.

He laughed. "I called hoping we could find some time." His tone grew softer. "It's so sad to have a family far apart like ours. I thought maybe you'd show me around, and we'd have dinner. I've never been here, you know. I'm as excited as a kid. Cannery Row and the sea lions and all."

He hesitated.

"That is, if you feel up to it after the strain of traveling."

"Of course I do," Sydney said gently. She ached to laugh. What a travesty this was! My dear southern cousin to the husband I never had! Let us have a social interlude —speak of families and visit sea lions. I, who am about to be convicted of murder, will entertain you!

His voice was exultant.

"That's the best news ever. Should I rent a car?"

"Oh, no," she said quickly. "Mine is right here. Give me a minute, and I'll pick you up at the airport."

"Can Mr. Cross come along?" he asked.

"No," Sydney replied, her mind already on clothes. "He's out of town. It's only four. We have time to do the Seventeen Mile Drive before Cannery Row and dinner on Fisherman's Wharf."

"That sounds heavenly," he said. "In a few minutes, then."

Calling Ted Cross was almost an afterthought as she started out the door. What if Ted called and couldn't reach her? What if he or the attorney needed something from her?

The secretary's voice brought back a remembered resentment.

"I'm sorry," the girl purred. "Mr. Cross is out with Mr. Alexander until about five."

Sydney hesitated. "If Mr. Cross calls in, please tell him that Mr. Railland is here from Atlanta. We'll probably have dinner about seven at Lou's Grotto."

"Can he reach you in the meantime?" she asked.

Sydney hesitated. "I'm afraid not. We'll be sightseeing —the cannery and all that."

"I'll give him the message, Mrs. Fast," the girl promised.

Lee Railland, removed from the dolor of his mother's house, seemed to have expanded and taken on color.

He startled her with a cousinly kiss. "I declare this is a holiday . . . a new place to explore with my beautiful cousin."

Sydney laughed. "I have to adjust to all this southern gallantry, Lee."

"But surely Graham?" He looked at her searchingly.

Sydney caught her breath, remembering. "His was a different gallantry, Lee," she said quietly. "Perhaps more . . . European." Her voice trailed off. God. She must remember. How many times had John caught himself in half sentence like that, forcing himself to remember?

"I need to make just a long distance call before we leave," he said apologetically. "I've been trying since I called you. I'll try once more." He winked at her conspiratorily. "To assuage my conscience."

She watched him inside the phone booth. When he glanced toward her she imagined that he was speaking of her. Paranoid, she defined herself angrily.

"There." Lee came from the booth briskly. "We are ready to play. Where do we start?"

"There are wonderful choices," she said. "I like the Seventeen Mile ride. That would give us time to talk."

Having warned herself against slips of the tongue, Sydney dreaded the hours ahead. Her fear of long silences was ungrounded.

He chattered, asking her about her travels with Graham, talking of places he meant to go. When he said, "Take my wife," Sydney stared in astonishment.

"You're married?" she asked, regretting her undisguised astonishment.

He flushed with embarrassment. "Not yet. But I have plans."

He was in love, Sydney realized wryly. This mother's boy of a man had been smitten, but that made the conversation easy. "Tell me about her," she invited.

All love stories sound the same, Sydney thought ruefully. He stumbled a lot, describing the woman as "pretty" and speaking of her lonely years of widowhood. He was a blend of his mother's sharpness and his Aunt Flossie, endlessly sentimental.

He seemed unaware of his surroundings, the curve of sea coast, the woods of the Del Monte Estates, Cypress Point and Spy Glass Hill.

But as the sun slipped lower, this voluble little man lost steam, winding down like a mechanical toy. His face was morose as sunset flamed across the sky.

After failing to rouse him, Sydney herself fell silent as they neared Monterey. The sunset's fading colors slid in jagged streaks along the incoming waves.

"It's darker than I thought it would be," Sydney admitted as she pulled into the lot. "Maybe we should have looked at seals first."

"There's still enough light," he protested almost fiercely. "It's been a beautiful afternoon, this light."

She glanced at him, pondering his disjointed speech. Fatigue, she decided as he opened her door. It had been a long day for him, too.

Across the water from them, Sherman's Wharf was lit for the evening. Sydney saw the silhouettes of fishermen seeking the inevitable squid of those waters.

With Lee's hand companionably under her elbow, they walked down the wharf, past the military box to the end of the pier, where the sea lions sprawled in contentious indolence, barking and shoving and jockeying among themselves. Below in the water, brilliant in the dying light, a scarlet Portuguese man-of-war drifted sensually. A stab of anguish struck her. Like Wagner, but the man-of-war lived.

"The seals are all colors," Lee commented, peering at the crowded water.

"I think it's age," Sydney said absently. "Some of them look corroded, as if with time."

As Lee's hand on her elbow tightened, she glanced up in surprise. But he was not looking at her. He stared back to where her car was parked, to the street they had left, watching a trail of boys on bicycles pass with shouts.

Only one other person was still on the pier. The tourists had wandered off to the parking area. A woman walked slowly, lounging down the boardwalk toward them.

"Something the matter, Lee?" she asked.

He smiled at her with satisfaction. "There's nothing at all the matter now." Then he laughed softly. "You haven't asked me how I got your number?"

Sydney stared at him. Fast. Her phone was listed under Fast. It was not even in John's name. "Listing a phone is an invasion of privacy," he had said tersely. "List it in your name if you wish." S. J. Fast.

She would have stopped, but Lee prodded her forward, a hard stub of metal ramming in her ribs where his hand had caught her elbow in that gallant gesture.

"You just walk now," he said softly. "Just walk out to

the sea lions—like you suggested, Sydney Fast."

As she struggled for breath, he spoke again, his voice harder.

"Don't make a mistake, Sydney Fast," he said ominously. "That is one loaded gun. A single word—a single move I don't order, and it's over *that* fast."

As she glanced back, the failing light played tricks on her. Even the other walker seemed to have been swallowed up by the buildings along the pier. The metal prod hurt cruelly, but the gentleness of Lee's voice was more terrifying than a shout.

"What is it?" she asked in a whisper. "What do you want?"

"Just move, cousin," he said softly. "Keep moving to the end of the pier." But he laughed. "Funny you should ask. We intend to do some living, my girl and me, and for that we need our money back—the Hastings money. That's all we want."

"My God, Lee, John tried to give it back years ago," she said, remembering.

Lee Railland sneered. "That was just a trap. We were too smart for that. This way it's sure."

Sydney's feet were leaden, but his words forced her on. "We're going to stand here, Sydney Fast, looking at those seals. Funny how much darker it gets all of a sudden when the lights go on, isn't it?" His voice had developed a vibrato; sweat gleamed across his face. And fear.

"John," she said suddenly as he forced her nearer the water. "You killed John."

He shook his head. "We're in it together," he said smugly. "I located you, of course, by tricking that attorney Alexander. But together we managed the blabbermouth in Chicago. With John gone, there's only you."

165

He peered intently down the pier without loosening his grip on her.

"We haven't made any mistakes, and we don't aim to," he said, smiling into her face again. "Your husband made one mistake in not knowing the Hastingses well enough. 'A Hastings' word is as good as the wind it blows away with,' my mother always said. You remember my mother, don't you, Sydney Fast?"

She stared at the terror in his eyes that matched her own. Was it terror or madness, she wondered suddenly. The other Graham Hastings. Lee kept saying *we*. Then the devil that was the other Graham Hastings was here too.

"Lena— Did Graham Hastings kill Lena, too?" she asked.

Her words caught him off guard. "Graham?" When he laughed the gun moved unsteadily against her rib cage. "Good Lord, Graham's been dead for years. Hotheaded bastard that he was. Got knifed in a tavern brawl in the forties. My Clara killed that maid of yours. She had to. She went to pick her up, and damned if Lena hadn't found an old newspaper clipping of Clara—from that murder in Chicago that started the whole thing. She was onto Clara, the Jensen woman. She remembered giving Clara a dozen chances to copy the key to your car, and how Clara had hung around after your husband died like she was looking for something. Clara had to kill her. She had no choice."

The water slapped under the wooden pier. Lee's body was so close that Sydney could feel his heartbeat echoing her own. Anyone looking out here in this dimness would only think they were lovers . . . that close.

Suddenly footsteps vibrated along the pier; Lee's gun

was a sharp pain in her side. His breath rasped. "Now," he cried harshly.

The barking of the seals drowned her cry. A pale pillar of light shone from Lou's Grotto as Sydney heard the softer voice.

"My God, Lee, we can't wait forever."

Sydney whirled toward the sound.

A woman stared back at her, smiling with a wide lush mouth. There was so little light. Sydney stared in disbelief. It was the woman from that old newspaper in Chicago, the same wide-spaced eyes subtly changed. That had been Clara. This woman's face had been impressed on her somewhere else. It had been at her own gate at Big Sur. The car stopped there to let Lena off and Sydney had been watching. Pilar. This was Lena's friend Pilar, like the Clara in the paper, but older, a little more florid. Pilar was Clara.

"That's right," the woman said, reading Sydney's astonishment quickly. "The other Mrs. Graham Hastings." Then her tone sharpened. "Don't chicken now, Lee. Get it over with or you'll miss that plane."

The sound Lee made was something like a whimper. He was so near that Sydney could feel his muscles tighten for what he was about to do. Tightening her shoulders, she tried to twist free of the hard pain of the gun pressed into her side. She almost got free. He was off balance, wrestling with her unsteadily on the slimy surface of the dock.

Pilar's voice was sudden and strident, and Sydney was concious of a heavy musk scent as the woman seized her. Lee swore softly, and a metallic sound like a distant explosion came from behind her. Pain angled along her leg, and she dived free of him, hearing the sharp burst of gunfire continue. There was a cry of astonishment as she slid free of their hands, plunging into the icy water. Nudged by an affronted seal, she floundered gasping and fighting for air.

The silence of the pier was gone. Like skipping stones, blips of gunfire struck the water. She dived again, feeling her wounded leg flowing blood into the thickened water as she floundered among seaweed and wires that appeared from nowhere to grasp at her clothes.

But there were other sounds: a hoarse scream, at once like and unlike Lee Railland's voice; gunfire buried in its own hollowness; and heavy feet vibrating on the wooden dock. The round bodies of the seals pressed against her as she groped for the pier's edge. As she caught the slimy wood in her hands, she opened her eyes. Beside her in the water, her face still glowing with life, floated Pilar. Dark strands of her thick hair swayed as the dead woman's arm rose slowly in a sort of salute, nudged upward by a grunting seal.

Sydney heard herself begin to scream. She clung to the edge of the pier, screaming as her throat flamed with pain.

She could never have lifted herself out. She knew that. Even when they tugged at her, she couldn't help, only rising with them as a dead weight, moaning helplessly.

Then she opened her eyes to see Don Sexton's face.

"You," she cried incredulously. "It's you."

There was no humor in Don Sexton's face. "I do seem to be Johnny-on-the-spot when you go for swims, don't I?"

"Lee Railland," she cried, remembering. "Lee and that Pilar. They tried to kill me."

"They're in good hands," he said quietly. As his

glance slid to the end of the pier, Sydney looked, too. A man in uniform was astride Pilar Loomis's body, performing without conviction the rhythmic rites of resuscitation. Sydney grabbed Don Sexton's arm for support.

The scene was a replay in her mind. She resisted the rhythm in her body without hope.

"Jesus," she said prayerfully. She tried to fix her eyes on Don Sexton, but she couldn't hold him still. She watched him waver there.

Flashlights moved on the dark pier. From the street the reassuring scarlet of a squad car light signalled brilliantly, and an approaching siren whined nearer. But Sydney could only stare at Don Sexton.

The brine of Monterey Bay returned to its own in hideous waves. Sexton waited helplessly, handkerchief in hand.

Sydney was crouching by the pier's edge, vomiting, when she heard Ted's frantic voice.

"Sydney," he was shouting. "She's all right, isn't she? Where's Sydney?"

"Just like always, right here," Don Sexton replied tiredly, handing her another handkerchief from somewhere to wipe her face.

Then suddenly it was Ted Cross who was supporting her and Ted's warm hands that gripped her own icy ones. The racking nausea abated at his touch.

20

As a child, Sydney remembered magic lantern slides shown in her parents' parlor, light clapping against her eyes like the opening and shutting of a strange unreadable book.

The night of Pilar's death brought her the same confused pain, as people and scenes flashed against her eyes, failing to register on her shocked consciousness.

Through the dressing of her leg and the pumping of her stomach, she felt Ted Cross, like a talisman, appearing and disappearing, standing at the ends of halls, and finally there beside her as they listened to Lee Railland's deposition.

Given a different chair, Don Sexton's office looked different. Lee Railland sat where Sydney had been so often. The old stenographer fixed his ferretlike attention on Lee's words instead of her own.

Lee's story was not pretty, lacking even the stature of tragedy. It was a hackneyed recital of a weak man transformed into a pawn by an unscrupulous woman.

Much of his story was startling to Sydney and to Ted, whose hand tightened on her fingers at Lee's words.

Graham Hastings had kept his compact with John without a backward thought. But he took with him into Mexico the woman Clara for whose love he had murdered and given up the Hastings inheritance. Clara insisted that they marry, not under the William Lowery name, but under his real name, Graham Hastings. Lee Railland had only Clara's word that Graham Hastings died in a tavern brawl in Mexico in the late forties.

Lee spoke with the gray slowness of defeat.

"The poor girl was penniless when she appealed to John Fast for money. He sent money all right, but he tried to trick her some way into a meeting. She figured he meant to stop her from bothering him forever. She was too clever for that. She set a trap of her own that he barely got away from."

"Were you in contact with Mrs. Hastings at this time?" Don Sexton asked.

Lee shook his head. "We only met a year ago," he said. "She came to me privately at the bank, trying to find the real William Lowery. She'd had searches made and decided maybe he had died."

A dumb look of pain crossed Lee's face. "It was like magic the way we felt about each other right from the first sight.

"From then we planned things together. When I discovered where John Fast was, she drummed up a friendship with the Jensen woman under the name Pilar Loomis.

"We figured we could pin John Fast's murder on his wife easy enough. With her gone, Clara could step forward as the real Mrs. Graham Hastings." He sighed. "If we'd waited, it would have come back to the family anyway. We would still have gotten our share."

"Then it was Clara Hastings, known as Pilar Loomis, who killed John Fast?"

He nodded. "She copied a car key she took off the Jensen woman and walked home across the fields so nobody would see her along the road that morning."

"The dog?" Don Sexton asked quietly.

"It didn't make sense to Clara that a man would destroy everything out of his past," Lee Railland said. "Clara couldn't get in to search the house because of that dog. She didn't want the old Graham Hastings story around to confuse the issue at Sydney Fast's trial.

"Was there such evidence?" Don Sexton asked.

Lee Railland nodded. "An envelope that the Jensen woman found, some personal stuff about an orphanage, along with clippings from the trial, with Clara's picture as big as life. When the Jensen woman confronted Clara with those pictures, Clara had no choice but to kill her."

"And the man in Chicago?" Don Sexton glanced at his notes. "Jim Ray Allan?"

Lee Railland's voice was spiritless. "Clara and I did that together because of what he knew. Or we thought he knew."

"You and Clara Hastings planned to kill Sydney Fast together tonight. Why?"

"She and that lawyer were snooping close—in Georgia at my family and then in Chicago. Then they advertised for the William Lowery man, whose name Clara and Graham had used. I was to fly back to Atlanta tonight under another name. The money would have just come back to us Hastingses then—me and Clara among the others."

A sudden energy animated Lee's face. It was hate. He

twisted in his seat to stare at Sydney, his eyes pale with loathing. "It should have been easy, but she was twisting like that. Clara moved in to help me and the gun slipped."

He shook his head as if to dislodge the memory. "Even after I heard Clara's cry, I couldn't stop shooting. My hand just kept pumping that gun. Not that it matters now." His energy spent, Lee slumped again in the chair, turning away. "Nothing matters now."

With questions still droning on, Ted tightened his hand on Sydney's and motioned her out. He drove her home to the house on Big Sur in silence.

Ted was no good at building fires. This astonished Sydney. He was annoyingly clever at everything else. "In the first place," she told him patiently, "two logs are not enough. You have to start with three. The one in the middle will catch from the draft."

"And the second place?" he asked acidly, when this requirement was filled.

"The paper," she explained. "You don't just wad it all higgledy-piggledy. You twist the sheets in the middle, like giant bow ties."

"You're going to feel pretty stupid when this doesn't catch," he warned her, setting his lighter to the collection of bow ties.

"You'll feel worse when it does," she laughed.

"I'm very good at following directions," he admitted as the lick of flames settled into a crackling burning among logs.

"And lots of other important things," she told him gently.

"Don Sexton is coming by when he's through," he warned her. "I asked him to."

173

"But it's over, isn't it?" she asked. "Isn't it really all over?"

"Nothing is ever all over, Syd," he reminded her. "You know that. Your marriage to John is a part of you like the past weeks have been. You are in the clear, if that's what you mean. Lee's deposition puts you out of the picture.

"Of course Lee will be brought to trial," he went on. "That will probably turn into a long and onerous business in spite of his confession. But at least his family will be well able to afford the legal expenses the way things have turned out."

He grinned at her puzzled look. "Surely you realise that the Hastings estate will be returned to the family now. Will that bother you?"

She shook her head. "How could it matter what happens to the money? How could anyone care after all the death and loss it has caused?"

He took her hands in his.

"There's also been a lot saved," he reminded her. "You could have died from Lee's bullets instead of Pilar."

"I was only trying to throw him off balance," she said distractedly. "And then he fired."

"Thank God," Ted said quietly.

"But Don Sexton was there so fast . . . and then you. I don't really understand all that."

Ted shook his head. "That was a combination of good luck and your careful upbringing."

At her incredulous glance, he nodded. "Right. Alexander and I spent one long day, alternately shouting and cordial, but long. John's arrangement with Alexander had been designed to keep the Hastings name and his

174

identity as John Fast separate. Somebody had gotten through that barrier . . . through Alexander. I really didn't know whether Alexander had slipped up with somebody else or with Lee Railland, who had told us that he handled that account."

He grinned at Sydney. "Let me just say that convincing R. O. Alexander that he has made a fatal mistake is not the easiest thing in the world. But finally he broke down. Last summer, the sixteenth of July to be exact, Lee Railland sent Alexander some documents requiring signatures. Railland was adamant that the documents be returned to Atlanta within days. Alexander, perfectly innocent of Railland's intent, sent them to John by messenger in order to have them ready in time."

Sydney looked at Ted. "A messenger?" she asked.

"A young law clerk—a man named Foster," Ted said.

Then she nodded. "A young man, long hair. He came without calling even. John talked to him in the study awhile, and then the man went away."

"It was a trap," Ted explained. "He was followed, probably by Clara. John Fast's cover was blown that day."

"It was after that that John put on new locks—took the trip to San Francisco."

Sydney agreed.

"John realized right away that he was vulnerable," Ted said. "He must have decided not to run. The trip was to his insurance agent for new policies on his life in your name."

"Then Wagner. In August or September he brought Wagner."

"John *must* have acted different, Sydney. You must have noticed some tension!"

She shook her head. "I thought he was getting paranoid. He said that all old men are cowards."

Ted shrugged. "I was still mulling over the information I got out of Alexander when we got the message that you were out with Lee Railland. Fortunately the girl was precise. She gave me the message word for word, including the cannery and the restaurant's name."

He grinned at her. "Too bad you didn't think to mention the Seventeen Mile Drive.

"I called Don Sexton about my suspicions, and he put out an alert for your red Corvette. He had that car pretty well in mind, you know.

"I guess that was one wild search down to Big Sur, out in the valley, through every corner of Monterey, but no red Corvette.

"After dark they found the car parked on Cannery Row, but *you* were gone. They started searching the pier almost too late. You know the rest."

Sydney shuddered. "I'll never drink water again. And seals are slimy."

"So are cousins," Ted added, grinning. "As I said, it was luck and your good manners in calling your plans that made it end well."

"But how did you get there so fast?"

"Wait till you see the bill for that chartered flight from San Francisco. Twenty-five minutes worth of fast air makes a real dent in the pocket money, my sweet."

"My sweet." Sydney picked the endearment from among Ted's bantering words instantly. She didn't look at him. What was wrong with her? How had John become a long-ago memory buried deep under the pain? At the thought of his name she felt only compassion. John fleeing the devil, John waiting for the inevitable end.

"And John fretted his Faust obsession all those years, Ted," Sydney said suddenly. "There was no devil except in John Fast's mind."

"I thought about that tonight while Lee Railland was telling his pitiful tale," Ted agreed. "Each of us selects a mythic role to play. John's myth was himself against the devil, born of the guilt of that original compact. Me?" he laughed shortly. "A graying attorney abandons his work to ride off as Lancelot serving his friend's queen."

"But successfully." Sydney smiled, then paused. "Who am I, Ted?" she asked after a minute. "The old Sydney Fast is past recovering. I don't know her. I'm not sure I even like her."

The clock in the hall—her clock and John's—tolled a slow eleven chimes into the sudden silence.

Ted rose, pulling her to her feet. "Maybe you're the girl who slept a long time behind the security of an enchanted fence?" he bantered. "Do you think you can keep food down by now?" he asked plaintively. "I'm starving."

The picture imprinted itself instantly behind Sydney's eyes. Maiden, hair bound by a gold circlet, one arm trailing from the couch. Rose. Her name was Rose. Beyond the thicket lay the real world of dragons and pestilence and the sordid humiliations of mortality.

"Starving," Ted repeated almost pitifully.

"Anything but fish," she managed to reply.

He looked pained. "Tough about the sole. Meuniere." He shook his head.

Of course he was kidding. The steaks Ted pulled from the refrigerator were still in a brown wrapper.

She watched him rub the salt with the cut garlic clove around the big wooden bowl.

"Anchovy paste," he ordered. "How can I make salad without anchovy paste?"

"Easy," she reminded him.

"We always eat steaks when you cook," she told him.

"Complainers are considered volunteers," he said airily, handing her a warm plate and her glass of wine. "And I thought I was clever getting these bought while you were getting your stomach emptied."

Sydney ate silently, watching the light glisten on her wine glass and hearing the sporadic crackle of Ted's fire.

Sexton joined them for coffee and cognac. "I know her brand," he told Ted, "having done this drowning bit with her before. But I have to admit," he said, raising his snifter toward Sydney, "I'm glad my original instincts were right about you."

"Now come on," Sydney said, almost annoyed. "You led me through hell barefooted trying to prove me guilty."

"You were all the suspect I had," Don Sexton said simply. "My intuition told me something was missing. I thought you were hiding the puzzle pieces. For that I apologize."

"Sleeping Beauty," Ted Cross said suddenly, out of context. Both men laughed indulgently.

The brandy turned the inside of Sydney's head to gold. Ted asked Don Sexton something about Lee Railland's testimony, and the detective began to talk, rocking back and forth on his heels. The men's voices rumbled companionably. Sydney's head whirled and she left them to go to her room and John's.

But the room was no longer hers and John's room, it was hers alone. She stared about, astonished at an evolution she had not observed. Only her own scent hung in the air.

The disorder was feminine chaos, pale clothes draped on the lounge, the white suitcase spilling silk on the carpet.

She wished suddenly that John could know how it had ended, that she understood the terror that he had lived with alone, his careful attempts to protect both of them against his past. The locks, the coming of Wagner, the silly insurance policies that had made her a natural suspect of murder.

Winter tapped at the windows. Once open, the wind rushed in, pasting her clothing against her flesh. She slid her hands down her body, along the curved line of her rib cage, the prominence of hip bones, remembering John's thumbs pressed against them with laughter at her thinness.

Out on the deck, the fog felt like the real sea. It swept about her in a tempest, chilling her flesh. Something hot and primitive rose in her throat. "I'm alive," she told herself triumphantly. "I'm alive and awake and I'm not afraid."

She clasped her body in her own arms and stood stubbornly against the whipping wind. The sea was their place—John's and Wagner's.

When Ted came looking he found her there.

He said nothing as he slid his arm about her waist. Against her chilled skin his hand blazed with warmth.

Winter would come early this year. The house was resisting the winds. Its foundation clung to the earth with stubborn man-made claws. But the wind was only rebuffed, not defeated. The river of fog reminded her that the wind would some day reclaim this hill. Manzanita and twisted pine would again cover the space that Sydney and John Fast had called their own.

"When will you leave me?" she asked Ted.

"Whenever you send me away," he replied.

"I will never be like that again," she warned. When he didn't reply, her words rushed on, trying to warn him. "I don't even know, Ted. I don't even know who I'll be."

"I'm a patient man," he said mildly. "And curious."